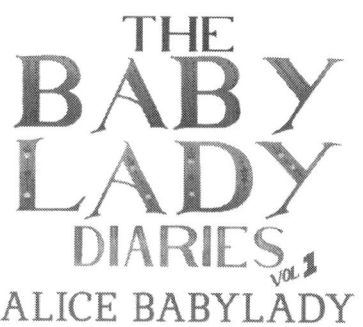

THE BABY LADY DIARIES

VOL 1

ALICE BABYLADY

D1795326

Note from Alice

Thank you for purchasing and reading The Baby Lady Diaries. By doing so you are not only supporting me (thank you!) but also in turn are supporting some very special charities.

40% of all profits from This Series will be donated to Tommy's The Baby Charity, Acute Neonatal Transfer Service and Norfolk and Norwich Neonatal Intensive Care Unit.

Dedication

Thirteen may be unlucky for some, but not for me. Thirteen is my lucky number. I couldn't love each one of you more.

Meet the Babyladys

My name is Alice and this story belongs to me. Here is a little bit about each one of the Babylady family members you will meet in Book One.

Alice Babylady — aged 28

Petite, curly dark hair, blue eyes, olive skin.

Mother of eight children under ten and wife to Henry.

Loves children, horses and reading. Addicted to Gü puddings.

Usually patient and calm but can, occasionally (regularly), be found with her head in her hands, muttering FML, FMFL and/or FFS.

Henry Babylady — aged 35

Tall, dark and handsome; typical alpha male.

Used to be a bit of a shit but, since having children, mostly now acts like a grown-up.

Ridiculously patient and laid-back.

Owns a commercial property development company.

Loves family holidays, dogs, and steak dinners.

Will avoid any organised activity that includes hordes of other people's children at all costs, once famously opting to spend his afternoon jet washing maggot infested wheelie bins instead of attending his godson's 6th birthday party at Bounce and Bowl Planet.

Martha Babylady — aged 10

Eldest daughter. Very gentle by nature.

A daydreamer with striking blue eyes. Caring and thoughtful, although a bit of a wind up at times.

Loves her pony and yoghurts.

Wants to have her belly button pierced and dye her hair white blonde (not happening!).

Margot Babylady — aged 8

Second eldest daughter. The curly haired comedian of the family, always has a prank in the pipeline.

Excellent company but a self-confessed lazybones.

Described by her class teacher as 'very funny but challenging', she has a very active imagination. David Walliams is her hero.

Nora Babylady — aged 7

Third eldest daughter. A Stepford housewife in the making.

Cannot abide mess, always brushing her strawberry blonde hair.

Once listed a duster on a stick at the top of her Christmas present wish list.

Alice pays her five pounds each week to unpack the family shopping and organise the kitchen cupboards and fridge.

Loves Lush unicorn bath bombs and giving Henry heart palpations by doing back flips on the garden trampoline.

Edward Babylady — aged 6

Eldest son. The blue eyed boy. Very kind and caring. Sometimes henpecked by the girls.

Football mad and VERY mischievous. Once got his head stuck in a banister and had to be cut free with an electric jigsaw.

Loves pepperoni pizza and Cherry Drop sweets. Wants a petrol go-kart.

Etta Babylady — aged 4

Fourth daughter. Black, bottom-length, curly hair and dark eyes. Best friends with Agatha, her younger sister. Always smiling and happy.

Loves playing with dolls, swimming, and dancing.

Very bossy, firm favourite with her school teacher due to her tendency to be a snitch and because she is very talented at reading and writing.

Wants to be a weather girl or a ballet dancer when she grows up because she likes the outfits.

Charles Babylady — aged 3

Second son. Curly hair and blue eyes. Extremely handsome.

Has a faint scar on his forehead from hitting his head on a swing set whilst pretending he was a flying dolphin.

Very tough. Always play-fighting with his brother, Edward.

Loves food — any food. Hates bedtime and having his hair washed.

Animal obsessed. Has an ant farm and a guinea pig called Norman.

Agatha Babylady — aged 3

Fifth daughter. Striking ringlet curls, very advanced for her age. Fiery personality.

Loves singing, dancing and riding her Shetland pony, Tinker.

Never without her bear, which she has had since birth.

Doesn't like going to bed; claims it causes her to have low blood sugar, bringing on dizzy spells which can only be rectified by a Blue Riband and another 30 minutes out of bed.

Penny Babylady — aged 2

Youngest daughter. Cute but extremely loud. Curly blonde hair and blue eyes.

Loves her blanket — 'the Yanit', Wotsits and anything pink. Doesn't like the word 'no'.

Favourite outfit is a pink princess ball gown, a purple 'Malia rocks!' baseball cap and polka-dot wellies, as worn to this year's Badminton horse trials — all day — after an epic, outfit-related tantrum/battle, which she won.

Ruby aka 'The MIL'

Family cat. Very aggressive tendencies which, according to her animal therapist, stem from her being an Egyptian slave in a past life.

Generally alternates her time in her current life between lounging in her radiator bed and launching unprovoked attacks on anyone who comes within striking distance.

Will not eat cat food, only tuna — preferably from the Seychelles and always in spring water.

Tara

Female family dog — Hungarian Vizsla. Purchased for Henry but favours Alice.

Very happy, docile and a bit dim at times. Can usually be found asleep on a footstool by the fire.

The boss of the canines in the household. Once got stuck inside a porta-loo.

Chubb

Male family dog — a Chow Chow. Bit of a weirdo, very loveable, ridiculously clever. Very obedient and polite.

Loves bread. If he was a human, he would be a vegetarian, bow-tie-wearing, university graduate.

Daisy

Female family dog — a Mastiff, sister to Nancy. Very quiet and tolerant, loves attention. Remarkably loud bark.

Incredibly scatty and with a tendency to lose control of her bladder when scared or excited.

Cannot swim. Extremely heavy to haul out of the garden pond.

Nancy

Female family dog — also a Mastiff. Daisy's litter mate. Possibly the world's most bolshiest dog. Definitely the greediest. Not at all obedient. Selective hearing. Food stealer.

Loves the children and acts as a chaperone to them. Sulks when told off.

William

Male Mastiff. Loves his family. Loyal and obedient, aloof

with strangers.

Alice has a particular soft spot for William — 'her special boy'.

Believes intruders should be eaten whole and that cheese is life.

Burmese

Holstein dressage horse. Big, strong and magnificent.

Difficult temperament when stressed.

Gentle with children. Doesn't like to be told what to do.

Loves carrots, drinking from puddles and rolling in mud after he has just been groomed.

Roman

Cob mare. Moody in the stable. Ancient and ideal for the children as very lazy and bombproof.

Gifted to the children from their riding instructor after they all learned to ride the mare.

Hard to catch unless there's food on offer. Worth her weight in gold.

Tinker

Agatha and Etta's Shetland pony. VERY fat and VERY naughty. Sometimes will nip if in one of his moods.

Escape artist. Top horse in the field. Often referred to as

'the Shitland'.

Star

The older girls' pony. Dust allergy so lives out with Tinker. Very kind and genuine little mare but scared of crisp packets and bikes.

Talented jumper and will stand for hours patiently munching a haynet while the children groom her and plait her mane.

Porker and Sausage

Gloucestershire pigs.

Love apples and belly rubs. Do not like having their food bowls taken away. Family pets who will never end up on a dinner plate whilst on the Babylady children's watch.

Norman

Guinea pig. Ginger. Strong sexual tendencies. Squeaks a lot. Lives with Etta's lop eared rabbit whose name changes as often as Etta's favourite television character.

NOVEMBER

Sunday 12th November

Isn't it funny how the days you expect to be the most ordinary sometimes turn out to be the most extraordinary...?

Last night my husband Henry and I came to the conclusion that we are both craving 'The Good Life' and so, with the optimism and clarity that only wine can provide, we have come up with a plan — we are going to sell our family home, leave our large, bustling village and relocate to a rural abode deep in the English countryside, taking with us our eight children under ten, two dogs, my horse and our mentally unstable cat.

***

Yesterday started like most mornings in our house. The standard 6 a.m. wakeup call came courtesy of Martha, Etta, Nora and Margot who had decided to stage their own live interpretation of *The Hunger Games*. This in turn had also woken up Penny and Agatha who were, no doubt, both keen to join in the battle that was underway in the playroom and had started trying to clamber over their bedroom door stair-gate. When that failed, they resorted to banging their juice cups on the wall to raise attention, whilst shrieking for rescue.

A mischievous yell of, 'Watch us, girls! We're going to jump off the book shelf!' confirmed that Edward and Charles, our two boys, were also awake. This prompted Henry to rush out of bed, shouting, 'Boys! Don't you dare jump! DO NOT DO IT! Stay exactly where you are. I'm coming to get you!' Thankfully, drama was soon averted and there was no need for another Sunday morning dash to A&E...

(The local walk-in emergency centre was surprisingly busy last time for 8 a.m. on a Sunday morning. The doctor was lovely though, laughing off my apologies and reassuring me that a toddler with a Tic Tac stuck up her nose was a welcome challenge after having dealt with mainly difficult, booze-fuelled patients since 11 p.m. the previous evening.)

Luckily my children are just like me — they love to eat. As soon as breakfast was mentioned, all chaos was halted and they eagerly made their way downstairs. We always have a cooked breakfast at the weekend so I started making rounds of sausage sandwiches using thick, hand-cut Tiger bread, oozing with butter and ketchup. I allowed myself a minute to enjoy my own sandwich before buttering another round of bread, waiting for the inevitable 'Is there any more, darling?' from Henry. After so many years together, I can read him like a book.

Amid the chatter and laughter I caught him glancing

towards the swimming bags I'd packed last night ready for this morning. I smiled to myself, knowing what was coming next. Over the sound of the coffee machine, Henry ventured, 'Alice... will you be okay to take the kids to their lessons this morning?'

'Why? Do you not want to come and watch?'

'Erm, well, yes, but... well, I just I thought I might get on with a few jobs around here and then get my hair cut as we're off out tonight. But if you need the help, obviously I'll come and lend a hand. I know it's a lot on your own.'

I looked at him, grinning at the way he was pleading silently with me with his eyes. I toyed briefly with the idea of making him come along but then let him off the hook and watched the relief wash over his face.

'It's okay. I don't mind if you want to stay here. Florence will be there and she'll help me if needs be.'

We have the same conversation almost every Saturday morning. Henry hates any arranged activity involving large groups of kids and listening to what he calls 'school gate tittle-tattle' and will always find something (anything) else to do in order to avoid being dragged along. To be fair, I can't blame him. Witnessing our children bobbing around in the local pool while their long-suffering teacher, Barbara, desperately tries to maintain some semblance of control, is painful at times. She seems to spend most of the lessons frantically blowing her whistle and repeatedly shrieking, 'CHILDREN! ATTENTION! LISTEN TO ME, PLEASE, CHILDREN!'

Despite nearly deafening me with whistle blasts every

week, I do occasionally feel sorry for poor Barbara. The little duckling swimmers couldn't care less about poolside time-outs, her NVQs in Pool Safety and Early Years Water Skills or her immaculate makeup (complete with signature coral lipstick and blue mascara/eye liner combo, the epitome of 1980's glamour). She generally has the patience of a saint but even she has her limits...

On one memorable occasion after a particularly bad lesson, upon returning from her 'thought-gathering fag', she gathered the whole class round for a meeting where she proceeded to threaten to have the leisure centre manager ban the whole class from attending further lessons. Clearly this was meant to strike fear and terror into their prepubescent hearts but the response to this was a mixture of eye rolls, laughter (children) and the odd remark of 'pull the other one, Babs, you bullshitting cow' (parents). We all knew it wouldn't happen.

The manager she was referring to was the painfully shy 22-year-old Jonathan who doubled up as a life guard. He wouldn't dare. Jonathan knows the score. He was there when Judy the receptionist refused to bend the rules and let Pamela — the Queen of the Mummy Tribe with her Gucci bag and academically superior son, Dudley Junior — redeem an expired voucher for a free sunbed session. When it became clear Judy wasn't going to back down and give Pamela her free six minutes, the situation got heated, her tribe descended on 'the jealous jobsworth' and as the saying goes, shit went down.

After what he witnessed that day, I am confident to say that without a doubt Jonathan knows better than to rub any of the Mum Club up the wrong way, so the chances of him banning all twelve children from attending Duckling Swimmers is as likely as my husband volunteering to give me a morning off and oversee it all solo. Not a chance in hell!

It's not all bad though. I enjoy watching my children learn a skill and having fun and if I didn't go I would miss out on all the mum chat, which is usually supplied by Linda from the hairdressers who has a son in Margot's class. Linda is one of those women who more often than not starts her conversations with, 'I shouldn't be repeating this, but...' or 'Between you and me...' I'm always curious as to where she gets her information because while she means no harm, I, for one, definitely wouldn't be telling her anything I didn't want repeated to most of the county. However, despite the rest of the village knowing exactly what Linda is like, she is always the source of all local gossip and news.

***

Sarah, one of my most sensible friends, had agreed to babysit for the evening so I was looking forward to a rare night off with Henry and was in a good mood. I breezed through the day, even finding 'mum is a willy' written on my bedroom door in black liquid eyeliner didn't bring me down. I was going out. OUT!!

Ever punctual, Sarah arrived at half past six and had barely taken her coat off before she was roped into judging a dance-off between my eldest girls — Martha, Margot and Nora. I managed to pull her aside just long enough to remind her where the snacks, first aid kit and fire extinguisher are and, no, I'm not joking! Margot currently has a huge and ongoing fascination with fire, thanks to the Fire Safety week at school. The fireman — who obviously isn't a parent — let Margot 'stop, drop, and roll' her Headteacher.

In total honesty, she is so obsessed I wouldn't put it past her to give one of us a shove towards an open flame in order to give herself the opportunity to put her newly acquired skills into practice. Five times this week alone she's informed me of the correct procedure for dealing with someone on fire. I listen, wide-eyed, as her excitement animates her voice while she repeats the step-by-step process that she will follow should one of us find ourselves on fire and how, once she has dealt with the situation, she will then telephone 999 to relay to the operator in a 'calm, clear voice' details of the event that has taken place together with 'victim's name, age, location and treatment received.' Each time I hear it I am torn — half proud, half terrified.

By the time Henry and I were ready to leave, Sarah had not only managed to get all my little people into their night-clothes without a single objection, she also had them snuggled up in the television room for story time. There she was with our youngest daughter, Penny, clinging around her neck like a monkey, whilst she read *The Lion, the Witch and the Wardrobe* to her captivated audience. They were all so engrossed that none of them even seemed to notice as we waved goodbye and left.

Nothing fazes Sarah — she is a secondary school teacher. Nerves of steel, that woman.

Henry and I walked the short distance to our local pub. The building is like many properties in the village, sitting quietly by the river, hundreds of years old yet immaculate. The garden is a beautiful place to spend summer afternoons with its private river frontage lined by willow trees and raised flower borders. In winter you are always greeted by the warmth of the two roaring fires and the smell of mulled wine but my favourite time to visit is the Christmas season. As soon as you walk through the entrance, you are hit with the unmistakable scent of a forest, courtesy of the fresh pine and larkspur garlands that the owners drape along the reclaimed oak beams that frame the bar.

The restaurant within the pub serves simple but good-quality food. The large round tables are always covered with pristine white linen and tall, clear vases bursting with seasonal flowers as centre pieces. That evening the vase on our table held a riot of freesias, gypsophila and thistles jockeying for space with jewel-coloured berries. Low lighting and the single white candle in a vintage Dom Perignon champagne bottle on each table made it the perfect setting to relax, eat well and enjoy being childfree.

After polishing off a starter and a main of bavette steak with roasted veg, served with the best creamy cheddar mash you will find anywhere, we retreated to the bar. We settled on a Chesterfield sofa close to one of the fires with a bottle of wine and chatted, enjoying the novelty of being able to have a conversation with each other that wasn't littered with half-finished sentences, interruptions and the background noise of a small army of infants. The topic of conversation soon became the amount of squabbling the children had been doing lately and then, perhaps fuelled by the wine or the atmosphere, Henry said it.

'I'm glad we came out tonight because there's something I've been wanting to talk to you about. I've been thinking about this a lot and the house really isn't big enough for us anymore. The girls need their own rooms and, to be honest, I'm sick of hearing the arguing which I think is mostly because of the lack of space.'

Turning towards me on the sofa, he continued in a rush, 'I think we should sell up! Find a bigger house with land, somewhere really rural with no neighbours. You can work from anywhere and I could make arrangements to work from home a few days a week.'

He was clearly serious. I could see it in his face as he stared at me, waiting for my response. I wasn't sure what to say… It was completely out of the blue. A frenzy of scattergun thoughts scurried through my mind, each clamouring for attention.

We love our house and the village we live in…

…Henry's most rural living experience to date is owning a Barbour jacket and pulling on a pair of Hunter wellies to walk the dogs. Would he really enjoy the countryside?

…I've always wanted to live in the country. Who are you if you don't dream of owning a thatched cottage with a country

kitchen complete with an Aga and a farmhouse dresser bursting with Emma Bridgewater?

Hang on... countryside also means horses...

I'd grown up pony mad. I was one of those girls who was always either burying my head in a Ruby Ferguson *Jill* book, watching *International Velvet* curled up on the sofa or at the stables riding. I'd always owned my own horses but when I had my children I gave up as I just didn't have the time. Regardless, to my delight, my children share my passion for all things equine. I taught them all to ride as soon as they could sit up and they spend most Sundays at Windmill Farm, the local riding school, owned by Jean, a friend of mine, who has kindly taken my beautiful dressage horse on loan to look after as her own. It means he's in good hands which is really important because despite being a really sweet-tempered boy, he can be a handful. It also means I can escape to Jean's yard for a few hours each week to see him. My older girls are always asking for their own pony but we have such a busy life it has never been a real option. The nearest I thought I would get to a house with land for horses was watching *Escape To The Country* with a coffee in one hand and a Hobnob in the other.

More to the point, now it's an option, do I really *want* to move? We've been happy and settled in our family home for many years. It's a lovely place to live, the kind of place where everyone knows each other and says hello. You always feel safe because of the real sense of community. Most residents on our road are either families like us with children or retired couples who've owned their property for many years. It's more of a town now really, having expanded with several new housing developments in recent years, and has everything a family needs — a family owned bakery, butcher's shop, an outstanding-rated Ofsted infant and junior school, a small supermarket, a hairdressers and a coffee shop. Would moving just mean we would be leaving all the things we love behind for a bit more space?

For the rest of the evening (after Henry assured me he wasn't having a midlife crisis and definitely wanted to give rural life a go) we mentally moved to the English countryside. We discussed in detail how we envisaged life in the country in a bigger house — I would get my much longed-for large family kitchen with an Aga and Henry could work from home a few days a week. This would mean we could have another dog join our family, which up until now had not been an option due to lack of space and time. Most importantly though, our children would have their own rooms and would be able to enjoy the freedom that acres of outdoor space would provide, which would hopefully cut down on the constant quarrelling between them.

Monday 13th November

We are actually going to do it!

Wednesday 15th November

We've both been grinning like idiots for the last few days and merrily browsing through Rightmove whenever we get five minutes. I haven't been this elated since I fit into a size 8 pair of jeans in Zara. Admittedly they turned out to be a size 12 on an 8 hanger but those five oblivious minutes were bloody amazing.

Thursday 16th November

Such a busy week. The kids are fully on board with the move — I think it was the promise of their own pony that did it! Henry has dealt with getting the house on the market, although choosing which estate agent to use wasn't without its dramas. After a few phone calls it was a choice between Reuben — a well-dressed, very posh, older gentleman with a double-barrelled surname who answers everything you ask him with 'yar' or 'one could' — or Dan who is more 'yes, mate' and from a smaller, local agency. Dan was my personal favourite, if only for the reason that he didn't really seem that bothered if we listed with him, or not so you didn't get all the usual estate agent hard sell. Despite what Henry would tell you, my favouritism was honestly for that reason and nothing to do with him looking just like Muggy Mike from *Love Island*.

Reuben came round first. I won't bore you with the details as anyone who has sold a house knows the drill and those who haven't are honestly not missing much. Long and short — he arrived on time, dressed immaculately. He measured, he complimented (standard estate agent patter) then excused himself, promising a follow-up call for our decision the following afternoon. A few hours later, Dan arrived, twenty minutes late and announced to me and half the street he was here to value my gaff. He slouched in, slipped off his loafers, narrowly avoiding the cat's claws as he brushed past her and went to look around. He was quite professional, despite him calling me 'babe' more than once and giving me the odd wink (which, given that he looked like a Greek god in chinos, I loved as much as Henry hated).

Then it happened. As my husband was mid-flow, discussing our extension, Dan's phone started to ring. For reasons known only to himself, Dan decided to answer the call via Bluetooth. If that wasn't bad enough, I found myself having to bite the insides of my cheeks and cough to disguise my laughter as he held his finger up at Henry in a 'give me a moment' gesture and actually dared to mouth 'shhh.' It got better. It seems that Dan is not *just* an estate agent. Oh no. He is, in fact, an estate agent who gives less than no fucks. As he mouthed 'shhh', he doubled it up with a 'be quiet' hand signal.

Before Henry had a chance to react, along came the icing on the cake — a stage whisper of 'Mate, this is a really important client, can you give me some privacy for a few minutes?' Presumably requesting that we both make ourselves scarce out of our own kitchen. Needless to say, that didn't go down well and Henry really wasn't keen to use 'Can you give me some privacy?' Dan after that. So Reuben, with his handmade shoes and his Mont Blanc pen, has got the gig.

Friday 17th November

The first viewing was a waste of time. I spent all morning cleaning up (how do children make so much mess?!) for the viewers to be here literally two minutes before declaring they didn't like the floor plan, that it was 'not their thing' and then left before even looking upstairs. Why do people not look at the particulars before viewing someone's home? It's so intrusive and annoying plus I had to cancel a coffee morning with Florence because of the appointment. I love mornings with Florence; she always has good cake. Good cake in my house never lasts five minutes.

Florence is one of my closet friends even though, on paper, you wouldn't pair us together. Firstly, she's ten years my senior and really posh. She's also a raging (and I mean raging) snob. She doesn't wear high street, she's all Hermes belts and crisp, white, Ralph Lauren and once described Nandos as 'vulgar'. She speaks just like Joanna Lumley and believes in 'leaving careers and money matters to husbands' but she is also hilarious. We clicked because we share a love of horses and she has the same dry, sarcastic sense of humour as me and can make me cry with laughter and, most importantly, I can trust her.

She's just called me and she's furious. 'Oh, hello darling,

have you heard!?'

'Heard? I don't think so, no. What's happened?'

'I've had some heated words after drop-off this morning with the lunch attendant, the tubby one with the red hair; it's quite disgusting, darling! That woman, THAT BLOODY WOMAN has been attacking my Frances's character and I just will not stand for it! She denied it all, of course!'

Allegedly, one of the school dinner ladies has been calling one of Florence's daughters 'a difficult, greedy and disruptive brat', although Florence didn't hear about it first-hand. The information came from her cleaner, who was told by her hairdresser who is... you guessed it! Linda. However she came about the information, Florence is now gunning for the dinner lady and said she is going to demand a meeting with the Headteacher on Monday and a formal apology as, in her words, 'I do not donate football kits every year, run the sweet treats stall every month and give my free time to the PTA to put up with this shit! She's picked the wrong mother!'

Knowing what I know about Linda, I tried to warn Florence not to go full throttle until she had all the facts. '*If* it was said, then it's terrible but maybe try to establish if it was said first? You know how Chinese whispers can be and you say this information came originally from Linda?' I then reminded Florence of some of the more outrageous things Linda has said which have turned out to be untrue...

Linda once swore to us all at swimming lessons that she'd spotted Emma Bunton buying toilet roll in the Co-op and had overheard her telling the cashier she had moved to the area. This caused major hysteria amongst the playground ladies, some of whom saw it as an opportunity to relive their youth. They started casually hanging out in the café opposite the Co-op Local, wearing the true '90s ensemble of Girl Power T-shirts and powder-pink tracksuits with hair in bunches, on the off-chance of bumping into the Spice Girl herself.

Dreams were shattered however, when the cashier was collared getting into his Ford Focus after his shift and was questioned by Pamela (Mummy Tribe Queen Bee) who was all set on becoming Emma's new BFF. It soon became apparent that Emma Bunton was, in fact, a blonde estate agent in her early fifties who had recently moved to the village and had crossed paths with Linda when she'd staggered across the road (Linda, not the estate agent) to buy a second litre bottle of vodka, four WKDs, and a bottle of rosé 'to get the party started' before heading for an evening at the local pub to celebrate her nail technician's birthday.

According to the cashier, Linda was VERY merry and had started gushing how much she loved 'zig-a-zig-ah' and then tried to encourage the village newcomer to accompany her to karaoke 'to show everyone how it's done.' This news travelled like wildfire, causing Linda to be the subject of the village gossip she usually loved to spread, especially as it later also came to light that Linda and co. never even made it to karaoke.

Ralph the Landlord told a few people, including Henry, his account of Linda and friends on the evening in question and his exact words were: 'They did come in briefly but, honestly, I just couldn't serve them on account of them all being absolutely shit-faced.' Linda later claimed Ralph was being dramatic because he saw her stumble in her high heels, although I doubt this is true. Last summer our neighbours' son, Tim, got sacked from his job at Halfords so, in an attempt to perk himself up, downed nine double Jack Daniels and cokes in about half an hour then promptly fell off his chair and proceeded to set his shirt sleeve on fire with a flaming sambuca. Ralph calmly patted out the flames with his bar cloth, gave him a pint of tap water, and casually said, 'Take ten in the beer garden, pal; get yourself together then come and have a beer,' so I'm inclined to believe that, if Ralph says you're too pissed to be served, then you most probably really are too pissed.

Florence eventually agreed with me and said she would speak to Linda before putting an official complaint in to the Chairman of Governors, so that's something.

5 p.m.

I'm so annoyed!!!

I have to do bath, story and bedtime then try to make the house look less of a bombsite before another viewing tomorrow (how do children trash a whole house in an hour?) on my own because Henry has decided today is the day to start getting fit and has sodded off to the gym 'to do some cardio, then have a swim and sauna' with his knobhead mate, Ian. Never mind that our house looks like we've been burgled and there are eight children that need bathing — you enjoy your swim, hun.

I probably wouldn't be as annoyed if it wasn't with Ian. I try not to be negative about people, especially Henry's mates, but I just can't stand this particular friend. Putting aside the fact he is rude and obnoxious, he spends every opportunity posing. You should see him as he pulls out his comb and runs it through his thick, black hair whilst lounging on the bonnet of his 'showroom new with all the extras' BMW M5, which he 'paid for in cash', winking at any woman who looks under retirement age that passes him. It's so cringeworthy. He thinks he looks like Tom Cruise in *Top Gun*. I think he looks like a twat.

He's also a bad influence on my husband. It's because of him that Henry missed his flight back from Las Vegas last year and got so drunk in London last Christmas that, despite them managing (by some miracle) to get the night train back home, they then fell asleep, missed their stop and connecting train, and, when they were finally woken up by rail staff when the train discontinued, Henry, obviously still having some vodka-based bravery, agreed to let Ian phone and wake me up at two in the morning to request I send them 'help as a matter of urgency.' The only information they supplied was they had no idea where they were but they 'could see a car park and a Costa Coffee with some gorgeous-looking sandwiches in the window, but it's shut.' I won't tell you my response; I will leave that to your imagination. And I'm not even going to get into our wedding day, the tattoo of a lion which looks like a Labrador in a wig, or Henry's stag do. All you need to know is that Ian is a fucking idiot.

8 p.m.

I do not believe this. I've made supper, bathed all the kids, loaded the dishwasher, cleaned the bathroom and got them all into bed and he is still not home! How is anyone at the gym for three hours? He's really taking the piss now. I've sent him a few casual WhatsApp messages asking when he's coming home and texted him a couple of times as well (in case he doesn't have Wi-Fi or 4G). I bet they've gone to the bloody pub. If Henry comes home pissed, I'm going to lose my shit. I *knew* something like this would happen; it's always the same when those two are together. Bloody Ian!

8:30 p.m.

Henry's home. All is fine; he's not drunk. I can confirm my husband is a lovely man and not really a waste of space like I portrayed earlier. His phone ran out of battery and he was late because he'd called in at Waitrose to pick up ingredients for Margot's school cooking lesson tomorrow (forgot I asked him to do that — whoops). He also came bearing gifts — a box of Lindt, some posh crisps and a Neal's Yard bath oil so I could 'have a relaxing bath, then put your feet up and watch those crap reality shows you like with some nibbles' to say thank you for managing supper and bedtime without him. Oops.

I feel a bit guilty now. I probably need to try to delete those casual messages before he reads them... Particularly the last few

I sent because they weren't overly casual if I'm being honest. I'm thinking now that I must try and have more faith in him. After all, I myself have had a few unfortunate alcohol-related incidents over the years and I do (if I'm being completely truthful) have a few friends who at times, as lovely as they are, have been known to encourage me to do some pretty irresponsible (although obviously hilarious) things after a few glasses of bubbles. So I've decided I'm going to try to be less of a nag and much more tolerant.

I still don't like Ian though.

Monday 20th November

We had two more viewings today. Henry is still refusing to let the Dan thing drop and I'm sick of hearing about it. He keeps telling everyone (including potential buyers) all about it and if that isn't bad enough, he refuses to call Dan anything but 'that fucking little dickhead.' I could have died with embarrassment today when he made Reuben pose as Dan to show our viewers — Mr and Mrs Davis — how he 'slung him out of the front door, shoes still in hand.' Poor Reuben. Judging by his face, I don't think anyone had ever grabbed him by the scruff of the neck before. I had to speak to Henry about it before the next viewing, informing him in no uncertain terms that I do not want a repeat performance!

In other news, Nora has nits, which means all the kids probably have them. You can guess what I'm going to be doing all evening. Thank God for Nitty Gritty combs. Makes me itch just thinking about it.

Tuesday 21st November

A busy but great day today. I got the children off to school, dropped Etta and Edward at pre-school and rushed back to finish cleaning the house which, with three under threes, was a nightmare. I somehow managed to change all nine beds and re-make them with my white Egyptian cotton sets. I'd ironed them meticulously last night and the finished result was more five-star hotel quality than my usual half-hearted 'I'm sick of doing this' efforts. Anyway, the house looked lovely, even if I do say so myself. I even splashed out on beautiful fresh flowers for every room... although I can admit now that it's possible I went a little OTT. Every room had an explosion of deep plums, rustic pinks, and cream winter peonies — I LOVE peonies!

We had a viewing booked in for two o'clock and an hour or so before Reuben was due to arrive, his number flashed up on my mobile screen. 'Hi yar, it's Reuben here,' he announced. 'I shall be with you shortly. However I need to confirm that it's okay for me to show a second potential purchaser around straight after Mr and Mrs Atkinson. They are in an excellent position, having exchanged and due to complete in four weeks.

Cash purchasers, just sold their excellent barn conversion — one of those eco projects, stunning views, slightly strange layout. Anyway, can I say yah to them? We would be out of your hair as soon as possible. However, I *am* aware you have school collection commitments?'

'Hold on a second, Reuben. I'll just check with Henry. I'll have to leave after the first viewing but Henry is here working from home today so I think that will be fine.'

'Yah, no problem. One could always rearrange for later this week but they are very keen so one should strike whilst the iron's hot.'

I found Henry working at his computer. 'Henry, Reuben's on the phone and says there's another couple wanting to view the house straight after today's original viewing. Could you either do the school run or be around for the second viewing?'

He looked up from his pile of paperwork and replied, 'Yes. That's okay; we may as well get them in today while the house is tidy because once the kids are home they'll demolish all the hard work and it'll be in a mess again before supper.'

'Reuben? Henry said that's fine. You can let your second viewers know they can come today.'

'Splendid! See you shortly! Bye for now!'

Henry turned to me as soon as I hung up. 'Do you want to get the children or do the viewing? In all honesty, I would rather not do the school run. I don't really want to be collared by Edwards's teacher again, not after the incident with the book bag and the class gerbil.'

I stifled a laugh. 'It's okay, I'll take the little three and go and collect the kids. You do the viewing; you know more about the extension and the garage conversion than I do anyway. Actually, I'll make myself scarce before Reuben arrives and call Florence. We could take a slow walk around the village and get a sandwich from the bakery.'

After the usual battle to get the youngest two children in their buggy, complete with the usual protests from Agatha (think buckaroo meets planking followed by the inevitable kicking off of her Peppa Pig wellies as a last-ditch attempt at defiance), I then had a ten-minute debate with Charles about the buggy board. I wanted him to stand on it. He made it clear he definitely didn't *want* to stand on it. The buggy board has become a real issue. Charles thinks he can walk because being nearly three means he's 'a big boy' and admittedly, yes, he *can* walk, but he walks so very slowly! We once were lapped by our neighbour David who's almost 70, walks with a stick and was on the wait-list for a hip replacement. He passed us just as we left our house then passed us again at the end of the next road on his way back home, carrying a bag from the newsagent's which is a good ten-minute walk for an able-bodied person. That's how slow Mr 'I'm-a-Big-Boy' is.

In the end, I applied the best parenting technique I've learned along the way of being a mother to eight. Bribery. I made a deal with him — a packet of Skips out of the cupboard as down payment and a pink-iced doughnut from the bakery as long as he stayed on the board on the journey there.

When the children and I got home, Henry had one of his smug-but-trying-not-to-be smirks pasted across his face. He was fairly evasive when telling me how the viewing went and answered with a vague 'time will tell' and I didn't have time to push him further because I had to get all the children ready for the monthly youth club disco. When I'd dropped the partygoers off and returned, I found Henry waiting for me at the threshold and before I even got to the driveway, he shouted with a huge grin, 'Guess what?! We've sold the house! Asking price subject to survey!' We did a happy dance in the front garden like a pair of teenagers and then went in and ordered a Chinese to celebrate.

I can't believe we've got a buyer! I never expected we would sell the house so quickly but that's what's happened. It hasn't sunk in yet but we'd better start properly looking for houses now. I wonder if it was the extra colour from the flowers or the Jo Malone candles that were throughout the house. Or maybe the roaring fires in the dining and living rooms that Henry had lit (there's nothing like logs crackling away on a cold and drizzly day to make you feel cosy). Whatever it was, the buyers decided our house was for them and they want a very quick sale...

WE ARE MOVING HOUSE!

Wednesday 22nd November

We've found the village we want to relocate to — it's called

High Acre. It's buried in deepest English countryside and it's like a time warp. You enter it via an old stone bridge with a brook running below and there's a village green where the community hold their annual summer fête. It's all cobbled lanes, thatched cottages and old stone houses and there's a village pub — The Fox — that's full of actual locals, a village hall which is home to the local WI and various other clubs and a village shop and post office complete with a red telephone box outside.

The residents sell home-grown produce at the front of their homes and at the end of their driveways, always with a little homemade sign and an honesty box. We originally found it last summer during one of the weekend adventures we love taking and fell in love with it straight away. I can't think why we didn't consider it in the first place. Henry said he feels like he's stepped into the set of *The Darling Buds Of May* each time we're there. Ideally, we want to be on the outskirts of the village but there's only one house for sale that's big enough and has land, an old farm-house. We are going to view it next week.

4 p.m.

I'm sorry to report that my cat is being a bit of a dick. Just back from the vet with her after she attacked Henry yesterday when she objected to him putting a shopping bag down on the chair where she was sprawled lazily dozing. Due to her confrontational personality traits, she has gained the controversial nickname of The MIL. Nick, our vet, has just confirmed once again that there's no medical reason why The

MIL is such a little cow. I just don't understand it. When she came home as a kitten, she was confident and cuddly (although admittedly a bit of a diva) and she never used to bite or scratch.

She's a seal point Birman with the most dazzling big blue eyes from which she stares regally at you. In fact, her whole demeanour is one of queenly indulgence, self-importance oozing out of her thick, shiny coat. Unfortunately though, as she's aged, she's developed a severe personality disorder, progressing from the odd, unprovoked swipe of the paw or a bite if the mood should take her, to full-on, unjustifiable, blood-drawing outbursts.

When her behaviour started to go downhill, I had her checked by the vet, thinking she must be unwell or have a physical reason to be so aggressive, but a series of tests confirmed there is nothing medically wrong with her. Having come from a reputable hobby breeder who lovingly raised her and her litter mates, left her mum at the Governing Council of the Cat Fancy (GCCF) recommended age of thirteen weeks and has only ever been handled carefully and with respect, allowed quiet time and not hounded by our dogs or children, we're perplexed as to why she's turned into such a madam.

She's a strange cat. She will sit on my lap happily purring for hours whilst letting me groom her then, out of nowhere, will just turn and sink her teeth into me. The MIL will not tolerate anyone else touching her, swearing and swishing her tail furiously at Henry if he even attempts to stroke her. Her only saving grace is that she doesn't go looking for trouble and gives the children a wide berth. She will live and let live and the children know not to touch her but if anyone is stupid enough to get close to her, she takes no prisoners, the dogs being a case in point. They're actually scared of her. She takes any opportunity to strike them and is very lucky that they're so good-natured and don't return the favour.

I've been trying everything to make her happier and less aggressive as, despite her quirks, we do love her. I've spent a small fortune on plug-in calmers, natural foods, quiet safe places, health tests... Our vet (who has been on the receiving end of her 'personality disorder' a few times) has suggested, as a last-ditch attempt, an appointment with an animal behaviour therapist and given me contact details for a lady who's registered to provide private home visits. I'm going to email her. Anything is worth a go.

Tuesday 28th November

I've been exchanging emails with Lizzie, the animal behaviourist. She seems a little bit 'out there' — claims to 'speak with the animals' — but however strange I might find it, Lizzie is confident she will be able to connect with Ruby to comfort her, build trust and then establish why she keeps trying to attack everyone. As much as I hope this is the case, I'm inclined to think 'good luck with that one, Liz!'

Florence, who knows a lot about cats as her family used to

breed Persians, is of the same opinion. She was still laughing when she said, 'Darling, that cat will never change. She's a terror and always will be but I look forward to seeing this woman in action. Good luck to her, I say! In fact, what day is she coming? This is a show I will not miss!'

I'm keeping my fingers crossed that The MIL is in a trusting and communicating mood when Lizzie comes tomorrow, although I saw her scratch the postman this morning as he tried to pat her when he walked past the garden wall she was sitting on, so I won't hold my breath.

Evening

I've just been searching for house-moving boxes and made the mistake of showing Henry how much they cost. He's now forbidden me to buy any and said he will go to the supermarkets and get some 'free of bloody charge.' I think he's underestimating just how much work it will be to get enough boxes for a house our size. I wish he wouldn't be so tight and just get a removal company to do it all.

Thursday 30th November

You wait until I see my bloody vet. Lizzie the animal behaviour expert has just left. I was right about Lizzie being a bit 'out there'. Despite it being minus two outside, she was wearing a long, floaty, purple, peacock-covered dress, a pair of battered sandals and a flower headband, all of which she later claimed was fair trade but the dress looked suspiciously like Monsoon to me. A quartz crystal pendant was dangling around her neck and she was clutching some organic herbal tea bags to her chest.

Henry, true to character, had escaped the appointment for a walk with our youngest three, as the rest of the little people were at school so the house was empty with the exception of Florence who had been looking forward to 'supporting me' so much that she had cancelled her weekly blow-dry, which in itself speaks volumes. Florence never misses her weekly blow-dry. She always says, 'A weekly blow-dry is just basic maintenance, Alice! There's nothing luxurious about self-care.'

Keen not to miss anything, she'd arrived straight after the morning school run with her Dior slippers in one hand and a packet of M&S chocolate shortcake biscuits in the other.

Lizzie sauntered straight into the sitting room and unpacked her therapy kit. I left Florence to make small talk while I made coffee and a mug of hot water for Lizzie's special tea bags.

I had barely got out the cups before Florence called through to the kitchen, 'Alice! Alice, darling! Could you come here? Leave the drinks for the moment. Lizzie has some important news for you involving the energy fields in the television room.' Even her upper-class drawl couldn't disguise the amusement in her voice and as I walked into the room, the smirk on Florence's face made me die a little inside. I knew at that point that this therapy was probably a huge mistake.

Lizzie wasted no time in getting me up to speed. 'Ah, Alice, there you are! It's the energy fields, my love — they're so negative, overwhelmingly so! We need to move the furniture around in here and unblock the flow. That's your problem!' She then closed her eyes and started muttering to herself. I couldn't even look at Florence.

'Are you okay there, Lizzie?' Florence enquired while shooting me a sly grin.

Lizzie slowly opened her eyes and started nodding into space. 'Yes, dear, I was just consulting with Cheyenne Arrow.'

'Cheyenne Arrow? Who is that, darling?' She was loving this.

'Cheyenne Arrow, my dears, is my Native American spirit guide... well, one of them. I am being advised by him as we speak so you're in good hands. Cheyenne Arrow knows his stuff although he senses Florence has a more open aura than you, Alice, so perhaps your friend could accompany me during my cleanse of the house and you relax here with your hot drink? Here's a thought — perhaps you would like to have a play with my prayer bowl?'

I've never seen Florence move so fast. 'Now, do tell me more about your other spirit guides?' I heard Florence say as they walked through into the kitchen. Lizzie didn't reply, she was too busy frantically swinging her 'knowledgeable pendulum' which she'd removed from her neck. She was pacing around my kitchen, muttering about heavy atmospheres and discussing (presumably with Mr Arrow) the rate at which my house was 'drinking up the frankincense oil' while she poured it onto her hands and launched it into the air, some of it landing perilously close to my Habitat furniture.

I politely declined the use of the prayer bowl and watched Lizzie and Florence disappear upstairs. I then sat drinking my coffee, thinking of ways to thank our vet for this recommendation. Despite his assurances that it was 'part and parcel of the job', he clearly harboured a grudge from when The MIL plunged her teeth into his hand at her last 'behaviour progress' meeting. That's the only possible reason I could think of for him to refer me to this lunatic.

Meanwhile, Florence had cheerfully followed Lizzie around my house and returned downstairs, this time armed with a cluster of clary sage which, as soon as Lizzie started to burn, absolutely reeked. Under her 'spirit guide's insistence', she placed several gemstones around doorways and re-arranged my mirrors and house plants. I had to draw the line at removing the television from the sitting room, which amused Florence even more than watching Lizzie drop still-smouldering herbs all over my dining room rug.

Being the ultimate wind-up merchant that she is, Florence then couldn't resist offering to help me 'pop the TV off the bracket' but I'd just about had enough at this point and snapped back, 'We are not taking my fucking television off the wall, Florence! Henry will go bloody mad! You know we had to pay for that to be hung!' After that, one of Lizzie's spirit guides must have sensed the tension so declared that turning the TV off would do.

Lizzie then announced she was ready to 'spiritually imprint and connect with Ruby' and plonked herself down on my carpet, ceremoniously laying out a feather, a large gold metal bowl and a small wooden stick while I went upstairs to find Ruby, who was fast asleep on my bed. I coaxed her down with a slice of turkey and she followed me into the television room. As soon as she spotted Lizzie sitting on the floor, she eyeballed her suspiciously. Florence, who had experienced The MIL in action on a few occasions, as a precaution, had slipped out of her lambswool 'house shoes' (slippers to you and I) and lifted her feet from the floor to sit, cross-legged, next to me on the sofa.

'Now, Alice, Flo, you both sit quietly, my dears, and I will proceed to start working with Ruby.' I inwardly laughed, knowing how much Florence despised having her name shortened but Florence seemed to be enjoying herself too much to mind.

'I'm so glad I skipped my blow-dry!' she whispered. After the TV comments, I couldn't resist replying 'Me too, Flo.'

'I must insist on silence, ladies, please. This is an important time, dears. My other spirit guide, Sam, is attempting to help me with Ruby and he is struggling, largely due to your energies.' That was too much for me and, as much as I battled, I couldn't hold in my laughter. I tried to mask it with coughing but it was met with a disapproving glance from Lizzie, the same glare a teacher would shoot a pupil who'd been caught giggling during assembly.

Once quiet was restored, Lizzie closed her eyes and started rubbing her stick around the rim of her bowl, making a loud humming noise. She stood up, walked over to Ruby, who was perched on the arm of her favourite chair and staring at Lizzie with a look of disdain, then held the humming bowl over The MIL's head. For the first few seconds, she seemed to be okay with it then out of nowhere, and in her usual fashion, she let out a furious hiss and turned with the speed of a Quarter Horse to take a meaningful swipe at the bowl, catching Lizzie's arm.

'AARRGGHH,' screeched Lizzie.

'Bloody hell!' boomed Florence.

'Keep calm, ladies,' Lizzie insisted. 'It's fine. Ruby is just letting out her negative emotions before she accepts my love and connects with me.'

I was speechless.

Lizzie put down the bowl, picked up the feather, and walked back over to The MIL. 'I will now show love to Ruby by gently stroking her with this feather that both of my spirit guides have selected for her.'

I knew what was going to happen so I tried to warn her. 'Lizzie, I'm sorry to interrupt you but I feel I have to tell you The MIL *really* doesn't like feathers. She had a toy with a feather and...'

Lizzie held up her hand dismissively. 'This is no ordinary feather, Alice. This feather has been blessed and cleansed by some very powerful spirit guides. Cheyenne Arrow was a village elder, chief, and warrior and that's without getting into his other lives. Also, Alice my love, Ruby has just told me she would rather you didn't call her The MIL so keep that in mind. *Ruby* has just given me permission to approach her.'

'Okay then, if you're sure, but be prepared, Lizzie. She's very likely to turn on you.'

Florence, clearly wanting her money's worth after missing her blow-dry, interjected. 'Alice! For goodness' sake! I am quite sure Lizzie knows what she is doing! This lady is not only an animal therapist, she is also a Reiki Master; she has a certificate, don't you, Liz?!' Lizzie nodded smugly and simply replied, 'Yes, Florence, yes I do.'

The next few minutes can only be described as carnage.

Ruby, it seemed, did not give a single shit that Lizzie was a Reiki Master or that she was approaching her with love and under the guidance of some 'very powerful spirit guides'. Ruby did, however, give lots of shits when Lizzie attempted to rub a feather along her body and expressed as much in her usual violent way. Perhaps Mr Arrow, the Native American, got confused and channelled his warrior battle vibes to Ruby instead of his calm and accepting village elder/chief ones, who knows. What I do know is that, by the time I managed to prize The MIL's teeth and claws from Lizzie's chin, I couldn't help thinking she resembled an Indian warrior chief herself.

'Maybe she isn't quite ready to accept help?' Florence kindly offered while watching Lizzie clean her wounds with witch hazel and tea tree.

Clearly not wanting to lose face, Lizzie replied, 'Yes, Ruby is indeed a very depressed soul with a lot of sadness. She just told me a story which caused her to lose control of her emotions. It all stems from her past life, this aggression you have just witnessed, it wasn't meant for me; she has nothing but love for me, but she just had to show me all about her previous existence. She was a slave in Egypt! I reminded her of her enslaver who she ended up murdering when she could take no more. That poor soul! She needs a lot of work but we will get there with a few more sessions. She's made so much progress today. She's feeling terrible and is sending me messages of her remorse and begging for forgiveness as we speak. She's mortified and devastated by her actions. I mean, just look at her — that's a cat in turmoil!'

Florence and I looked over at The MIL who was cleaning herself on the window sill. She let out a lazy yawn, stretched dramatically, then climbed into her heated radiator seat, padded the deep soft cushion with her paws until she was satisfied it was ready to receive her, and curled up for her afternoon nap. She didn't look like a depressed cat in turmoil to me.

'I have now officially heard it all,' chuckled Florence, out of Lizzie's earshot.

Florence and I helped Lizzie carry her bags to her car and said our goodbyes before standing together on my door step to wave her off.

'Well, that was bloody hilarious. What day is she coming

next week, so I can diary it?' asked Florence.

'You are joking, aren't you? I'm not having her come again!'

'Oh, you have to! This last hour has been the best entertainment I've had since I assisted Claire in burning all Richard's clothes!'

'Didn't you both get a caution for that?'

'No, we most certainly did not! The police only came as a precaution because a neighbour was worried the wind was going to change and he would lose his summerhouse, so he telephoned for the fire brigade. The police were simply present to ensure there were no breaches of the peace. They were mere bystanders, darling.'

'Well, I'm not paying that woman and her invisible friends £100 an hour for your amusement, Florence.'

'I will happily pay! This morning was brilliant! I cannot *wait* to tell my hairdresser. He's a massive fan of that alternative stuff; he always watches that show on Sky Living.'

'What, Cesar Milan?'

'No! *The Haunting Of...* with Kim someone or other. In fact, let's go and have a coffee and look it up on Sky Demand. We haven't had any of those biscuits I brought with me yet.'

'Come on then. Henry will be back soon so you may as well stick around and help me explain to him that we have an Egyptian murderer living under our roof and why our house smells like that dodgy vegan shop next to the library.'

Evening

I'm feeling a bit stressed about moving. It's the first of December tomorrow and the house is usually bursting with decorations by now but we've decided to just have one tree this year because we may be moving between Christmas Day and New Year's Eve. I think I'm possibly getting cold feet and wondering if we're making a mistake. I need to speak to Henry. Perhaps we need to pull out of the sale and forget the whole thing before we exchange. I was going to speak to him earlier but it wasn't the right time; he was too busy laughing about Lizzie's revelation of Ruby's past life as an Egyptian slave, amusing himself by consulting his spirit guides every time I asked him a question. He then downloaded *The Mummy* to 'try and understand Ruby on a deeper level.'

He's such a dick sometimes.

DECEMBER

Friday 1st December

I tried to speak to Henry this morning before the viewing at our potential new house tomorrow but it was impossible. The children were restless and kept bloody interrupting then the dogs needed to be walked so we all got wrapped up in an assortment of coats, hats and gloves and braved the wind and drizzle to stretch our legs in the meadow behind our house. Even in winter it's beautiful, fully encased by a thick perimeter of tall, aged oak trees that are so established and imposing they always remind me of *Alice in Wonderland*. The meadow is green, lush and full of wildlife all year round. The moment you reach the meadow via the opening in the trees, you feel like you've been transported into a different world.

The dogs ran ahead, disappearing in and out of the hedgerows, playfully chasing pheasants and the odd rabbit, all of which were too fast and too clever for my hounds to be of any threat; not that they are that way inclined. Both are far too busy bunny-hopping in an animated fashion through the overgrown grass, thoroughly enjoying the freedom of being able to roam and explore. So are our children for that matter, despite struggling to wade through the thick pasture which reaches (and, in some places, exceeds) the tops of their wellies. They were happy and giggling, their eight little faces flushed rosy red from the crisp, blustery day.

Henry and I exchanged knowing glances, holding hands and smiling at each other as we slowly strode along behind. I knew in that moment that we'd made the right decision. I'm glad I didn't bring up having second thoughts now. I think I'm just worried about such a big change for us all. I'm looking forward to seeing High Acre Village again tomorrow and looking at the farmhouse.

9 p.m.

I forgot to mention the boxes! After lumbering around all the supermarkets on his way home from work, Henry came in with a total of three boxes, one of which was a banana box with holes the size of my hand in the bottom. He clocked me looking at the boxes and we both laughed. 'I'll phone some companies tomorrow and get some removal quotes. I spent two hours looking for those boxes. Life's too short; if we book a complete pack-and-move deal, we can have a normal, all-singing, all-dancing Christmas here and then they can come after Christmas and pack it in one day and move us the next.' I smiled and the children cheered. Henry added, 'I know where all the decoration boxes are so I'll get them out of the garage in the morning. Then on our way home from the viewing, we can stop at the Christmas tree farm and get a couple of trees, I know how you love Christmas.'

I'm feeling much happier now and the children are so excited! I've just been online and ordered a wreath and two Christmas-style planters from Marks and Spencer's; a little bit over-priced but sod it! It's our last Christmas here; we may as well make it special. We're going to invite Florence, Adam, and their two daughters over for Boxing Day as well; we always have the best time with them.

Saturday 2nd December

Just home from the viewing. We both LOVE the farmhouse. It's located about three miles from High Acre Village so really rural and secluded. The only access is via a single farm track with deep ditches and lines of trees either side. They are gorgeous — the type that grow in a bend and meet in the centre to create an arch. It's magical and the views are perfect — open countryside and farmers' fields as far as the eye can see. There are no street lights and no neighbours so I can imagine it will be a bit spooky at night when Henry is away but it's not a deal breaker.

The house itself is tucked away out of sight behind a thick

hedgerow which also covers all the twelve-foot high, wrought-iron fencing that lines the perimeter. It's been empty for a while so it's all a bit overgrown and unloved. The bushes at the side of the electric gates have started to get out of control and are stopping them from fully opening so we had to park outside and push our way through. Once you're through the gates, there's a second, long, L-shaped driveway that reminds me of being a child and going to the local stables for riding lessons. The crunch of the gravel and the bumpy surface took me back to being five years old and I had the same excitement and butterflies in my stomach.

The farmhouse is huge, although I wouldn't say it's pretty... more extremely handsome. The brochure has a photo of it that I suspect was taken quite a few summers ago as, in the picture, there is a thick, deep, roof-to-floor blanket of purple wisteria bloom all over the front of the farmhouse. It looks like a postcard. There's hard standing all around the house and stables set back to the side, as well as a large garden sprawling all around and an orchard with mature fruit trees. Someone loved this house at some point, that's clear to see.

The gardens back onto five acres of paddocks and meadows and there are established trees around the boundary, making it completely private. A beautiful lake (more a large pond, really) can be seen from the living room windows and, to the other side of the house, there's a swimming pool set into the ground. It's huge but the paving around it has seen better days. The agent assures us that it's fully heated and in working order though and the kids would be in seventh heaven if they had their own swimming pool!

Inside is like a maze. There are so many rooms and doors... seven of them opening onto the garden on the ground floor alone. We walked through a huge, open-plan, country kitchen and day room with massive wood burner, a formal sitting room, dining room, TV room, office, utility and boot room — all with fireplaces or wood burners — and a hallway which is just never-ending. There are three toilets downstairs and an amenity door to a triple garage.

The rooms upstairs are enormous. It's at least three times the size of our current home and the ceilings are so high and grand. There are seven bedrooms, a few with en suites and a dressing room the size of my current bedroom, fitted with floor-to-ceiling, built-in wardrobes. The main bathroom has a Scar Face vibe — think black-and-gold, mirrored ceilings and a sunken jacuzzi bath. Henry loved it — typical man, he took a photo of it and sent it on WhatsApp to his friends together with the hashtag #callmetonymontana!

It needs a bit of work and a lot of love but it's perfect for our family and it's a vacant possession. Henry has worked our finances out and we can just about afford it. I hope we get it.

Sunday 3rd December

I can't stop thinking about the farmhouse! It would be such a special place for the children to grow up. As we were leaving I spotted an old wooden plaque on the gate that read 'Puddle-Duck Farm' which was buried under all the overgrown plants. I couldn't think of a better name.

8 p.m.

All the Christmas decorations are up so our house looks welcoming and Christmassy but I feel a bit detached from it now, like I've been cheating on it. I think my heart has been left in the middle of the English countryside, inside a slightly shabby but completely magical farmhouse.

Tuesday 4th December

Offer accepted! We are over the moon. It's all starting to feel real. We took the children to visit the High Acre school this morning. The journey was a complete nightmare. Last time it took us just over two hours. This morning, with five of the children (Florence looked after the youngest three, thank God), it took nearly three hours including two toilet breaks, an emergency car valet using baby wipes and a complete child wardrobe change in a Burger King car park due to Nora developing a sudden case of motion sickness.

When we (eventually) got to the school, we fell in love with it immediately. It's essentially a bungalow with a secure door as the main entrance, painted buttermilk yellow, nestled right in the heart of the village, opposite the family-run local shop and next to the picture-postcard village green. It sits in its own grounds with a large playing field and a playground which has 'words of kindness' written on the tarmac. This is such a lovely idea — a positive word has been chosen by each member of the school and has then been painted on the floor by the caretaker. A Christmas tree bursting with tinsel and flashing, multi-coloured fairy lights and a Nativity scene greeted us in the entrance.

We were met by Mr Plait, the Headteacher, a large, jolly man who finds everything funny which, given he is also going to be Margot's class teacher, is very reassuring. He took us on an all-access tour and we saw everything from pupils dressed as Rudolph, practicing for their annual pantomime, to messy play sessions in the reception and year one classes, where Etta and Edward will soon be spending their days. We also listened in on the older classes who were all engrossed in their winter-term topic — Ancient Greece.

Despite being a combined infant and junior school, there are only just over 70 pupils and so it's very personal and welcoming. We even met the school cook, a lovely old lady called Mary who was baking up a storm in the kitchen. The smell of her jam tarts cooling was enough to make my mouth water! All the staff were so friendly and chilled out. The children spent an hour in their new classes and judging by the chorus of praises and general excitement coming from the back of the car on the way home, I feel confident that the new schooling arrangements met the kids' approval as much as they do for Henry and I. The tiny class sizes alone are worth moving for.

Before we headed home, we took the children on a little tour of the village. It was a perfect English winter day, still and bitterly cold. It really is a chocolate box village. It occurred to me, as we drove over the bridge and passed an old stone cottage with a white picket fence before turning down the long country road towards the farmhouse, that our new home could be straight from the film *The Holiday*.

9 p.m.

Just back from the stables. I had a chat to Jean about Burmese. She is fine with me having him back from loan; turns out he's becoming too strong for her and has been skittish in traffic. She also offered me one of her riding school horses, a mare called Roman. She means a lot to me as I've known her since I was a child and my children also adore her, having all learned to ride on her. Jean has said she feels Roman needs a quieter life and some pampering and attention as she's approaching 30 years old which is perfect for us. My girls can gently hack her a few times a week to keep her active and Burmese will have a field companion.

Jean has also really kindly offered to transport them to the farm a few weeks after we move in which should give us time to make sure the fencing is secure, get the stables up to scratch, and ensure the paddocks are ragwort free. It's all coming together. She also has something in mind longer term for the children on the horse front. SO excited!

Monday 9th December

I forgot to say, it turned out that the dinner lady did say everything that Florence's cleaner told her she did. After Linda swore she was telling the truth and explained exactly how she knew (another dinner lady overheard it being said and told her), Florence stormed to the Headteacher's office and demanded action. The head (no doubt anxious not to lose his sports kit funding!) called in both the accused dinner lady and the one who claimed she heard the comments and shortly after, the accused fled the school in tears, having admitted she'd said all the things repeated.

Her reason for saying such nasty things about a child? Florence's daughter had dared to put her hand up and ask for another portion of apple crumble and custard at lunch. That's all! Quite shocking really. She was sacked and rightly so. I don't like to see anyone upset but she had it coming in my opinion.

Friday 14th December

Henry took Tara, our Hungarian Vizsla, to stud today to meet a beautiful boy called Stanley. The pairing has been a long time in the planning and the result of every health check known to man (or dog), about a thousand hours studying pedigrees and hundreds of emails between Henry and Lesley, Tara's breeder.

The plan was for us both to leave as soon as we got the children off to school. Henry and I had a bit of a debate over whether or not it would be easier to move three car seats from my car to his Range Rover or put one dog boot grate into my car. Henry opted to move the car seats, despite my opinion being the opposite. We agreed I would take the older five children to school and Henry would move the seats over and get Charles, Agatha, and Penny in the car together with Tara in the boot and be ready to start the hour's journey to Debbie (Stanley's owner) and Stanley.

As I turned the corner into our road I could hear Henry before I could see him. It sounded like a bad comedy act. 'For Christ's sake… Penny! Take that out of your mouth! Agatha… AGATHA, do not push that button; that's for the hand brake! Right, that's your last warning. Get out of the driver's seat. Charles… CHARLES! Oh, just go in, you little…'

'Daddy! We do not use bad words! I'm telling Mummy that you were going to say a bad word!'

'No, Daddy wasn't… I was going to say, "You bad car seat," and we don't need to tell Mummy. Have a Blue Riband out of the lunch box and sit down. Where's Charles? CHARLES?! Agatha, where is your brother? What do you mean, he's trying to get in the wheelie bin? CHARLES??'

'I'm not in the bin. I'm here, Daddy! Look, look at me! Look, I've got my dinosaur costume on!'

'Take it off! RIGHT NOW! I told you not to put it on. If you take it off, you can have a Blue Riband. Come on, you know we are going…'

'Mummy!!' chorused all three children as they spied me coming up the drive.

'Did you get them transferred over yet?' I asked, looking at Henry who was red in the face.

'No, I bloody well haven't. The kids have been playing up and these car seats are awful; they just won't do back up! These stupid clips just will not open; they must be faulty.'

'What, all three of them? No, they're just all in the recline position; they need to be upright for the clips to unlock.'

'Stupid bloody design. I bet they've had heaps of complaints about them.'

'They won the Mother&Baby Awards for best designed car seat.'

'Well I know a crap car seat when I see one and these are CRAP!'

After we got the seats fitted, the kids safely strapped in and Tara settled in the back, I locked up as quickly as possible, conscious that time was getting on. I climbed into the passenger seat and said, 'Right, I think we are about ready… Have you put the postcode in the sat nav?'

I knew by Henry's face that he had done it again. 'Slight problem… I can't recall where I've left the key fob.'

'You do this every time, Henry! How hard is it to look after one thing?'

'I was stressed with the children. It can't be far. I'll have a look inside.'

Half an hour and a few colourful words from both of us later, Henry finally found the key fob on the passenger seat of my car; he must have put it down as he took out the seats.

The children had soon got sick of waiting and had demanded to be freed from their seats and go inside the house . Penny had fallen asleep watching *Dora the Explorer* and Agatha and Charles were happily playing shops, dressed as a ballerina and a dinosaur. I looked at the three of them. 'I don't think I'll come now, Henry, not after all the stress. They're happy playing now and Penny is asleep.' I thought of the epic tantrum Penny would have if I disturbed her nap and shuddered.

'Right, okay then. It's probably for the best to be honest because, if we hit any traffic, we might be late for school pickup. I'll be off then. I'll text when I'm there … Sorry about losing the key.'

'It's alright, don't worry about it. The children would probably have been bored anyway so maybe it's worked out for the best. Let me know when you arrive safely.'

With Henry gone and the children happily amusing themselves, I used my time wisely. I made myself a coffee and drank it while it was still hot then posted a picture on Instagram of our other dog, Chubb, wearing reindeer antlers and my scarf. After this, my thoughts drifted to High Acre, so I downloaded *The Holiday* to watch it and compare the cottage and village it was filmed in to our new village and home.

I only managed to watch about ten minutes of it before all hell broke loose in the playroom. Agatha had launched a toy shopping trolley at Edward after she felt he had short-changed her on her purchase of a plastic chicken. The screams woke Penny and so that was the end of my me time. At least I got a hot coffee though.

4 p.m.

Glad I stayed here now. Henry has only just left so I would have been late for school home time. From what he said on the phone, it seems our dog is a complete hussy. Apparently, she didn't even play hard to get and he was ashamed of her. All being well, we should have puppies around Valentine's Day. Who says romance is dead?

Thursday 20th December

School broke up today. We've arranged to keep in contact with all the children's close friends though and are planning a reunion party once we're all settled at the farm.

We all went to the village Christmas fayre this evening. Just as I was feeling all nostalgic about it being our last ever time attending and reminiscing about all the previous events, Mr Simpson, the school grounds-man, who had landed the part of Santa, tripped over a chair leg mid 'HoHoHo', staggered and then clumsily fell off the stage and landed on top of the Guess How Many Sweets In The Jar stall.

His dramatic fall was witnessed by most of the village

children and the whole year one class who, moments before, had been lined up and ready to sing 'Silent Night', dressed as angels. They all looked on horrified as the most magical man in the world desperately attempted to reattach his beard while muttering 'bollocks' and 'oh, fucking hell' in a thick Home Counties accent. Martha told me on the way home that he smelt like Henry's friend from cricket, Ralph, which, if true, explains the staggering off the stage. Ralph drinks brandy like most people drink tea or coffee.

It wasn't all bad though — the children had a great time and I won a Dove gift set and a litre bottle of Cinzano. Not my usual tipple but, taking into account I have three solid days of Henry's mother coming up, I welcomed it with open arms.

8 p.m.

I think Henry may have been on the Cinzano! I was just enjoying five minutes peace while the children occupied themselves with throwing the reindeer dust that they won at the fayre around their bedrooms when Henry came in and sat next to me on the sofa. He had the look of someone who had something to discuss but would rather not be doing so. 'Darling, you know Marcus?'

Here we go… 'Yes, Henry, I remember Marcus, as I expect do most of our guests at my birthday BBQ last year. It's hard to forget a topless man wearing a pair of Barbie sunglasses, on all fours, pretending he is a zebra and attempting to eat a rose bush.'

'Oh, let it go, will you? I've told you so many times. He was on antibiotics and he doesn't usually drink spirits.'

'What about him anyway?'

'He's having a stag do on the 29th and I just thought I would mention it before anything was booked.'

'What, the 29th of January? Where is he having it?'

'Well, no, that's what I wanted to have a chat to you about… It's in Amsterdam and it's this month. I wanted to ask, if I did go, would you be cool with it? Or would you be sending me ranty texts every five minutes and inviting Florence over to help you burn all my clothes?'

'We move on the 28th December Henry! And Amsterdam! Really?'

'Yes… I know; that's why I'm asking now… What do you think?'

I smiled. 'Henry, how long have you known me, darling? Like you even need to ask.'

Friday 21st December

Henry isn't going to Amsterdam.

Monday 24th December

I love Ocado home shopping. The drivers are all always so polite and happy! After reading this morning's delivery receipt,

Henry's mood was more Victor Meldrew than 'Ben driving the apple van.' He did his usual loud, disapproving tutting then the running commentary of his thoughts whilst he read the receipt out loud at the top of his voice, in case I'd forgotten what I had ordered or Gail across the road wondered what goodies we had in for the Christmas season. 'Are you mad? ARE YOU BLOODY MENTAL? This is a ridiculous amount of food for three days. Five tins of Quality Street, Alice! All these boxes of biscuits? All this meat? Two organic turkeys, a beef joint, lamb, and two free-range chickens… For three days, Alice?! It won't even fit in the fridge. What on earth were you thinking? This is not the same list I saw last week!'

'DON'T YOU DARE raise your voice at me, Henry! You're the one who invited your parents to stay for two nights and three whole bloody days! Your mother also informs me that she's bringing your grandma. Florence and Adam are coming on Boxing Day with their children and, in case you've forgotten, Henry, we've got eight children of our own. What do you want me to do? Buy one chicken and a packet of shortbread and stretch it out over three days and eighteen people? Fine! Take it all back and you can cook for everyone. I'm just about sick to death of you! And if your mother dares start moaning because I didn't get a goose after last year…'

'Okay, OKAY, I'm sorry… I know, it's better to have too much than too little… but sixty Old Spot sausages, Alice? As well as all the bacon and breakfast pastries?'

Why do people say, 'Sorry, but…?' Luckily for my husband,

little ears were present or he would have got a two-word reply starting and ending with an F.

2 p.m.

Henry has gone to collect his parents and his grandma from the train station. The girls have been making sausage rolls and Charles and Edward have barely moved from the PlayStation all day. I managed to move the sofa bed into Henry's study for Ethel (grandma-in-law) and, much to Martha and Etta's irritation, they've been evicted from their room and put on a blow-up bed beside Agatha and Penny's cots to make room for the in-laws. I was going to put the in-laws in the boys' room, which would have been much easier, but last time Beryl, Henry's mum, made a massive fuss, saying the green, light-up dinosaurs on their ceiling gave her migraines. A lot of things give her migraines including, but not limited to, cheap orange juice, low thread-count bed sheets, having to be nice to dogs, cats, being nice to people...

Which reminds me, I must warn the children not to call the cat The MIL or tell Beryl that we have a cat named after her... It was a close call last time when Nora forgot herself and called out, 'M-I-L, come and get your food!'

Luckily, Martha spotted her sister's error and saved the day by shouting, 'Yes, come on, Ruby!' And did a really animated cat face and let out a loud meow. Beryl gave us all a withering look, eyed the plate in Nora's hand, and said, 'Oh, how ridiculous to feed a cat tuna steak!'

6 p.m.

Scrap that last entry, I hope they do tell her, the bloody cow. There should be a law against mothers-in-law staying at Christmas.

I knew she was in one of her moods as soon as I saw her, face like thunder, waiting for Henry to open the car door. She emerged from the car like the queen ready to receive her people, wrapped in a black, floor-length fur coat, her white-blonde hair — her 'Princess Diana do' Martha calls it — freshly set. I could smell the Youth Dew she doused herself in from ten feet away and she wasted no time before sniping at Henry, 'Don't just stand there; assist your grandmother!'

Poor Clive (Henry's father) attempted to lug Her Ladyship's vast suitcase up the driveway whilst having his orders barked at him like he was a naughty toddler. 'P-i-c-k up my luggage, please! One does not drag vintage Louis Vuitton! You know better than that, Clive!' She pronounced 'drag' as 'drahg' and 'please' as 'purlleess'; stupid, stuck-up snob.

Beryl's first words to me were not, 'Merry Christmas,' or, 'Where are my gorgeous grandchildren?' Instead, she stepped past the threshold, rolling her eyes at the 'Baby it's cold outside' door mat and 'Welcome to Christmas with Babyladys' wooden door sign and cast a judgmental eye around the hallway, turning her nose up at our fairy-lit, fresh garlands wrapped around the banisters, wrinkling her nose at our eight-foot tree decorated with an assortment of homemade decorations that the children have made over the years and said, 'Good God, where are my sunglasses? I thought you might have been a touch more understated with the decorations for once, Alice, all things considered.'

'What do you mean, "all things considered?" Your grandchildren decorated that tree you're turning your nose up at, Beryl.'

She looked at me with a death stare and spat back, 'I mean, as you are selling my ancestral home, the one that's been in my family for over 40 years, I thought you might have given me my last Christmas here without having to endure being blinded by Blackpool illuminations. That's what I mean. Although at least the tree and garlands are real. I suppose that's something... But that poor tree; it looks like it's in need of a good drink. Did you cut the base, Henry? Clive, get some water for this poor tree!'

I resisted the temptation to shove her into the Fraser fir and, instead, reminded Beryl that Henry and I had been paying a mortgage on 'her' home for the last eleven years and therefore it was actually 'our' home and, if she felt that strongly about us selling it, she should have purchased it back from us via our agent at the asking price, just like we did from her over a decade ago.

That seemed to shut her up.

11 p.m.

The kids are only just asleep! The excitement and anticipation for the big man in red, combined with the new bedroom arrangements, meant they messed around for hours so I've only just got into bed as I had to get all the presents in order under the tree and the birds in the oven on low. I can't wait to give the children their two main presents tomorrow — they are going to be *so* shocked. I also had to re-wash Beryl's sheets then tumble dry and iron them as she claimed she can now only use a certain washing powder (which she presented me with out of her suitcase). She claims she has skin allergies, which is fair enough, but a heads-up before eight o'clock at night would have been nice. Still, I did it… Not that she said thank you obviously.

Sarah phoned this evening to wish us all a happy Christmas and to tell me her news. Her boyfriend asked her to marry him! I am over the moon for her and she said his mum cried with happiness when they told her the news. I wish I had a mother-in-law like Sarah is going to have. Carol is lovely — she calls Sarah 'the daughter I had always dreamed of having' and I bet Carol doesn't criticise constantly or shoot her judgy looks left, right and centre.

Beryl never has anything nice to say about anyone. I've tried with her; I really have. For her birthday this year, Henry and I booked a weekend spa break for her and a friend. I put all the details in a card on top of a hamper containing a new White Company dressing gown, some cashmere slipper socks, and an ESPA bath and body oils set, had it wrapped nicely and then sent it recorded delivery. She didn't acknowledge it when she received it or a week later when we all went out for dinner… Says it all really; can't say 'thank you' for her Aveda spa break but can find time to say that my new batwing top made me look like a 'homeless Romanian Gypsy.'

25th December — Christmas Day

I felt like I had barely closed my eyes when I was woken with a jump by a chorus of excited voices.

'It'sss Chrissstmasssss!'

'He's been! He's been!'

'Look at all the presents!'

'He's left magic footprints!'

Henry and I both clambered out of bed, yawning and calling down to the children to wait for us before diving into their presents. We both then shared a little giggle and wished each other Happy Christmas as we pulled on our dressing gowns, grabbed our slippers, and made our way downstairs, overhearing their excited conversations in full flow.

Before we went up to bed last night, Henry had put his boots on and stood in some baking flour that I'd poured into a paint tray. He had then walked from the hallway fireplace to the dining room fireplace, where we had left their eight sacks of presents. I'd then helped him carefully put his feet inside plastic bags, unlaced the boots and removed them, creating a pretty magical scene for the younger children that Santa had appeared and walked snow through the house before disappearing back up the chimney.

Martha, although being the eldest and a 'non-believer', in

her usual gentle and sensitive way joined in the excitement and pretended to be as delighted as her siblings while giving me a coy smile and whispering to me out of ear shot of the others, 'Brilliant idea, Mum; they're so happy!'

Our guests had yet to surface so we shared a special family moment together, all scattered sitting on the rug around the fireplace in our dining room as each child, in age order, took it in turns opening presents while Margot and Martha made a note of who received what and from whom so we could write thank you letters on Boxing Day to post the day after (another of our family traditions). The children were delighted by all their gifts, ranging from toys, clothes, and Nora's favourite — Lush bath bombs — to new riding boots and jodhpurs.

I had kept Henry's until last. One of the things Henry is looking forward to doing when we move is making the most of the clear dark nights that the countryside offers, using a telescope. I had zero knowledge of telescopes and I really wanted to surprise him with one so had spent quite a few evenings over the last month researching them and seeking advice from companies that make them. In the end I'd purchased a pretty special one by all accounts by Bresser Messier, which I'm told is like buying a sports car lover a Ferrari.

The company owner assured me the model I had chosen wouldn't disappoint. It all seems very high-tech — amongst many other things, it takes the user on a tour of the solar system. Henry is notorious for not really being excited about presents so

I wasn't expecting the reaction it got. As soon as he tore back the wrapping paper, his face lit up. He then spent the next ten minutes telling me it was exactly what he wanted and what a clever and perfect wife I was while muttering words like 'brilliant' and 'exceptional' as he buried his head in the user guide. Worth every penny just to see him so elated.

I was also thrilled with my gifts. I received a set of Emma Bridgewater that I'd been stalking online since we'd exchanged on the farmhouse, my favourite perfume, and a selection of books I had on my Amazon wish list, perfect for me as I love to read. My favourite present though, was a drawing of all of the children. Henry had commissioned a local, very talented, artist; it was so thoughtful and something I shall always treasure.

Once we'd opened our gifts, Henry started unwinding all the toys from their packaging wires. I really believe toys are packaged to never be re-opened.

Our guests had, by this point, joined us, clutching their morning coffee and teas, eyes still squinting, obviously not used to being in the middle of bedlam five minutes after waking up.

I could hear Beryl complaining about the Christmas songs album we had playing in the background. Not wanting her to dampen my jubilant mood, I decided to take all the children upstairs to wash and dress them. It's a daily task I have down to a fine art. As I turned the taps on our modern bath and poured in some bubble bath, the children took turns to push the LED light menu to select which colour they fancied illuminating the bath. After much debate they settled on red 'like Santa's outfit.'

I run bath times like a military operation and Christmas Day was no exception. While Penny, Agatha and Etta played happily, splashing and giving each other bubble beards, I set the temperature in the shower for the older three girls who then took it in turns; one in, one out.

Before too long the bath had been emptied and refilled and was occupied this time by Edward and Charles and their Action Man figures. I sat in the hallway on the floor and plugged in my hairdryer to start blow-drying six heads of hair, one at a time, while keeping an eye on the boys.

They're a real girl gang, my daughters. All of them were snuggled in their fluffy dressing gowns, talking excitedly about the presents they'd just opened and the day ahead. Henry came up just as I'd finished blow-drying Etta, the last in line, and, after washing and dressing himself, he helped the boys get dry and dressed. I quickly showered then joined the rest of my family. We all stood together in the kitchen as I made a start to a breakfast fit for a king — sausages, bacon, eggs, fried bread, hash browns, as well as pastries and fruit.

Beryl walked in for another coffee and stared at us. 'What on earth have you all come as?' she asked, shaking her head. Every year we all wear festive jumpers and this year was no exception; all of us, including Henry, were a sea of matching reindeer jumpers with flashing red noses, and green elf slippers. We looked completely ridiculous and we all loved it.

***

'Right! Coats on, everyone!' It was just past two o'clock.

We'd not long had our lunch and Penny was having a rest. Henry's grandmother had also 'retired to her chambers to recharge.' Clive and Beryl (no doubt in need of a rest themselves after enduring eight hyperactive children who'd eaten their weight in selection boxes in between breakfast and lunch) had agreed to keep an ear out for Penny while the rest of us popped out for an hour.

'Ooowwhh we're playing; can't we stay here? We don't want to walk the dogs!' grumbled Martha who'd been engrossed in her fashion wheel for a good hour and had little intention of moving.

'There's plenty of time for that later on. Come on! Wrap up! It's cold out. Put your wellies on and your wax jackets. Let's go!' said Henry.

After a few more huffs and puffs, they all relented and began wrapping up ready to head out. Henry and I tried to act cool and pretend it was just a casual dog walk on Christmas Day in the rain, as you do.

'Shall we call in and say Happy Christmas to Jean as we're passing?' Henry casually asked me, trying to disguise his smirk as we trudged down the lane leading to the riding stables.

'Yes, we may as well do,' I replied, which was met with some deep sighs and eye rolls from the children.

'Oh, Mum, we all really want to go back home. I'm cold and we want to watch *The Santa Clause*. It starts soon!' Martha complained.

'Yes, it's Christmas. Why are we walking the dogs on

Christmas Day?' joined in Nora.

'Girls, it won't take long. Come on! Let's just wish them a happy Christmas and we can head home,' Henry cajoled as we all reached the entrance to the stables.

We walked into the spotless yard and were greeted by a line of brick stables with a row of horses' heads poking out. At the end of the line was a face that never failed to make me smile. Burmese, although not fond of the cold, looked content despite the frost on the ground, in his heavyweight stable rug complete with neck cover. He, along with a few of his stable friends, nickered as he saw us approaching (no doubt in the hope we came bearing treats). We all made a fuss of him and Edward told him all about his new, soon-to-be home.

We then turned into the indoor American barn which also held the pony stables. As planned, Jean and her husband, Colin, were waiting for us and holding two ponies decorated with tinsel and groomed to perfection; a piebald Shetland pony called Tinker and a bay Welsh pony called Star. Next to the ponies were two bright yellow, ride-on toy tractors for Edward and Charles. I've never seen the children so excited. They shrieked, they screamed, and hugged each other, then us, then Jean. They haven't stopped saying thank you since. I will never forget their faces today when they realised the ponies and tractors were theirs to keep.

This move is going to be the best thing to happen to us, I just know it.

Thursday 27th December

Tomorrow is moving day! Currently lying on blow-up bed in an empty shell that this time yesterday was our sitting room. It's so weird seeing our home bare, our family photos down, our rugs rolled up, all personal traces gone. I cried this afternoon when we took photos of the wall in the playroom where we've marked and dated the heights of each of the children on the first day of spring each year.

Henry has been a lot less emotional and, after calling me 'a mentalist', reminded me we can make a new height wall and that we're leaving in order to be able to make more memories as a family. It's still sad though. The removals came at lunchtime and packed everything apart from the bare minimum we need to get through tomorrow. The children also seem unaffected. Despite being a sea of hands and feet entwined on three double air mattresses, they're zonked.

I really can't believe we move tomorrow. We had a brilliant Christmas; a lovely end to our time here in this house. The in-laws and Henry's grandma left this morning although Beryl was still blanking Clive after it all kicked off yesterday.

Florence and Adam came for lunch with their two girls as planned. We had a really fun day. I made a huge roast for us all then we all played board games and demolished cheese boards while the children inhaled all the Quality Street (the ones Henry said we would never get through) and had a carpet picnic of sausage rolls, cheese balls, sandwiches, and a token bunch of grapes.

Beryl had been her usual critical, demanding self, making snide comments about my weight gain. 'You should probably admit defeat, Alice, and start buying a size twelve; you're not doing yourself any favours.' She wasn't too bad though once Florence arrived. Thankfully she has a certain way of shutting down such dickish behaviour, usually with a superior stare and one-liners like, 'Oh, do shut up, Beryl. You're in danger of turning the atmosphere as sour as you are, darling,' and so, on the whole, it was a successful day.

Around tea time, the children came downstairs, wrapped in bed sheets with tea towels on their heads and paper scripts in hand and announced they had a show to perform. Together they'd written their own version of the nativity. All of us adults sat beaming as we watched our little people confidently perform together. Even Nora, who is generally painfully shy, joined in, supported by her co-stars. It made me so proud of them all and, without sounding like a saddo, really made my Christmas.

We rewarded our little stars with a massive round of applause followed by hot chocolates with marshmallow spoon stirrers, After clocking yawns coming from them all, Florence and I decided to take both our broods upstairs and get them into PJs, brush their teeth, and get them settled in bed watching DVDs. By the time I checked on them half an hour later, they were all fast asleep.

With the children safely tucked up and the baby monitors on, the adults gathered around in the dining room to play a murder mystery game. In the hours that followed, the adults, who'd been drinking wine conservatively most of the day, really went to town on the booze, with the exception of Beryl and I; me on account of deciding there needed to be at least one sober, fully capable parent in the house in case one of the children should wake up or an emergency occur and Beryl on account of her being too furious that Clive had dared to have a drink and enjoy himself. She was also seething that Ruby had bitten her as she attempted to shove her off her cardigan that she'd left on the back of a chair.

It was getting late and the evening was just winding down. As I'd been up since six, I was finding it hard to keep my eyes open. Adam and Florence had decided to stay on our air bed for the evening. Just as Henry and I were discussing where to inflate it, Henry's dad staggered to his feet and clinked his whisky glass with a candlestick.

'Before we all get off to bed, I would like to make a speech,' he slurred, swaying slightly as he held onto the fire hearth to steady himself. Beryl's eyes set on Clive and she stepped towards him, grabbed onto his arm, and said 'For goodness' sake, DO NOT show me up any more than you already have done! Sit down, you stupid man.'

Clive, who most probably was sick of being told what to do in front of his family and their guests, cut Beryl short. 'No, Beryl, you sit down dear,' he replied calmly, but with a coldness that took the whole room's breath away. I had never ever heard him answer her back. He gently put down his glass on the table and, as Beryl tutted and lifted the glass and replaced it on top of a coaster, he continued to address the room.

'Right, as I was saying before, I *am* going to say a few words. Firstly, I would like to say thank you to Alice and Henry for having us to stay. And thank you especially to Alice for the meals she's prepared for us all; the ones which, knowing my wife as well as I do, will without any doubt be slagged off to all and sundry over the coming week. To be honest, as we're amongst friends, I don't mind saying I have about had it with her. I don't even want to come home from the office to her most days! I mean, who would? You see, my wife is truly awful to be honest with you! Forty-odd years of pure misery I've had with her. Thank goodness for golf, that's all I can say. On that note, let's all raise a glass to my son, Henry, and his wife, Alice, and TO HER NOT BEING A LIFE-RUINING BITCH!'

You could have heard a pin drop. Henry's grandmother Ethel was the first to speak. 'I knew we shouldn't have come on this cruise. Nothing ends well at sea; just look at the Titanic!'

We all looked at each other, speechless. Ethel, despite her age, was always sharp as a needle. No one said anything but I could tell we were all thinking the same thing.

Henry, prompted by my dagger stares signalling him to do or say something, was the first to react. He lent down by Ethel and gently said, 'Grandma, you're not on a cruise ship. You're at my home. You know who I am, don't you? Henry, your grandson? Do you remember? You came on the train?'

She looked at him for a few seconds with a vacant

expression and then scrunched up her face before letting out a howling laugh. 'Of course I bloody remember, you soppy git. I'm not senile yet! I was just making light, given the current situation. I got the idea from an episode of *Doc Martin* last week, you bunch of goons. Now do get up off the floor, you're leaning on my foot.'

Everyone belly laughed. Everyone, that is, apart from Beryl. She had already quietly left the room. Despite her chipping away at Clive relentlessly and her constant snipes to me and everyone else over the last few days, I couldn't help but feel sorry for her. I left everyone to get themselves organised and into bed. Clive had decided to sleep on the sofa and was already snoring, with Chubb lying on his feet.

I quietly got out a china cup and saucer and made her a cup of tea. I walked up the stairs, deliberately missing the third step — the creaky step it's become known as — took a deep breath and tapped on Beryl's door. 'It's just me. I've brought you a tea up. Can I come in?'

After a few moments came a quiet reply. 'Yes, you may.'

I ventured in, closed the door behind me and placed the tea on the side table. Beryl was already in bed wearing her Wallis nightie she'd been given for Christmas. With a Martina Cole book in her hand and her reading glasses hanging on a chain around her neck, she eyed me suspiciously. I hovered at the end of the bed. Despite knowing her for so long, I didn't feel comfortable sitting down.

Wanting to give her some kindness, but not quite sure of

the response I would get, I decided to try. I did for a second consider giving her a hug. No, that wasn't a good idea; she never even cuddles her grandchildren let alone the woman who she once openly stated 'was not, and never would be, good enough for her son.'

'I'm sure Clive didn't mean what he said. He's had a lot to drink. If it's any consolation, Florence just told Adam she wants to get a full-time job, so you know they're all talking rubbish. Everyone talks crap when they've been drinking. Henry's said some very hurtful things over the years. It really is just the booze. I believe, without doubt, Clive will be mortified in the morning.'

She looked back down at her book and replied, 'Yes. Possibly so, time will tell. Thank you for my tea.' I took that as my cue to leave so turned to the door, thinking perhaps I may see a slightly different Beryl going forward. She very quickly put me right.

'Good God! Will you ever learn how to make a palatable cup of tea, Alice? This is awful. You may as well take it away with you. I cannot drink this,' she spat as she held out the teacup and saucer and glared at me like I'd attempted to infect her with the Ebola virus.

I've now accepted she will never change her ways and I am no longer going to take it personally.

Friday 29th December

We are in our new home and it's everything we've been dreaming about and wishing for but it's been a long day. The removals arrived at 8 a.m. Henry had lost his shit by 9:30 a.m. due to me agreeing to let Jon and Jack, the removal men, pack up our coffee machine. Henry came downstairs and stopped dead, looking at the space where the coffee machine had been twenty minutes before.

'Alice, where is the machine? ALICE!' I joined him in the kitchen along with all the children who were sitting on the floor eating breakfast bars and sipping orange juice out of cartons. They'd been up with the larks, jumping around and running from one side of our empty house to the other, excited to eventually go to our new home and choose their new bedrooms.

'It's been packed, hun. I've kept some instant out and the kettle. Shall I make you a cup?'

'I hope you're joking, Alice! You know I can't drink instant! We discussed this! I told you I would take the machine in the car with me.'

'Well, it's packed now. I didn't think there would be enough room. Just have some instant. I've got a good one; Florence said she drank it when her machine went up the wall for the best part of two weeks.'

'What does Florence know about fucking coffee? She only bloody drinks it here, you know she's a tea drinker usually. No, I just can't drink it. Go and ask them for it back please. You know I need at least three cups to start my day, especially one as busy as this is going to be.'

'Firstly, do *not* swear at me! And, secondly, you're out of luck. I can't ask for it back as they've just left so it's this or a Capri Sun I'm afraid,' I said, holding up a jar of coffee to Henry.

'I DO NOT BELIEVE THIS! I cannot cope with instant!'

'Can you hear yourself, shouting over a cup of coffee? You're as bad as your mother, you snob.'

Henry glared at me and then erupted into a laugh. 'Sorry, darling, I'm just a bit uptight about today. I'll survive. Sorry for raising my voice.'

'Have you had a final look around upstairs to make sure we haven't forgotten anything?' I asked.

'Yes, there's nothing left. Feels so strange, doesn't it?' Henry replied.

Before I could respond, my mobile rang.

'Yar, Alice, Ruben here. I call bearing good news. Your sale has completed. Mr Dennison shall be along any moment to accept the keys from you both. I have been informed by your solicitor that you will be met as arranged at your new property to give you the keys at that end.'

I felt like crying for a second. As much as I wanted to move and had already fallen in love with our farmhouse, we were leaving a home that had given us some very happy memories. I turned to Henry.

'Henry, the money has gone through. The new owners are on their way now for the keys.'

'Are you there, Alice?' Ruben prompted

'Sorry, Ruben, yes I'm here. Just a bit taken aback... It's a big moment for us; feeling a little nostalgic thinking of all the memories I'm leaving behind in this house,' I replied.

'I understand, although do not lose sight of why you started this process. You are all about to live your dream. Memories are people, not places, Alice, and you are moving to a fantastic property.'

'Yes, you're right. Thank you for all your help, you've been brilliant.'

'Most welcome, Alice. It has been my pleasure. Do drop me an email when you're settled and let me know how you're all finding country life?'

'We shall do. I think the new owners and my friend have just arrived so I must go but thank you once again.'

'Yar, bye for now.'

'Bye, Ruben.' I gave Henry a look that said I wanted to sob but was trying not to then one of my favourite voices boomed and echoed through the empty hallway, diverting my mind.

'Darlings! Are you all ready? Your purchasers are outside waiting for the okay to start unloading.'

'Hello, yes, we're in the kitchen, Florence, and as ready as we will ever be.' Florence glanced at me and gave my arm a squeeze as she passed me in the kitchen. No words needed; she knew how I felt.

'Right, let's get this show on the road! Who wants to come in the car with Aunt Florence?' Eight hands raised in the air.

Monday 31st December — New Year's Eve

I have just unpacked our last box. It feels like we've been here forever. Without meaning to sound mental, I truly feel like I've been here before. I have such a contented, familiar feeling in this house; it's like supper with an old friend.

On our first morning, we all sat at our new, huge, oak kitchen table eating breakfast while watching a deer family graze around our pond. We couldn't have had a better start. It's so quiet here and I've seen a robin on our outside table every day since we arrived. I love robins. I've seen more wildlife here in a few days than I have in my whole lifetime. Despite being bitterly cold and in the depths of winter, our garden is alive. Hares dart across our paddocks each morning; swans and ducks that have made a home on our pond huddle on our floating island; and last night Henry and I saw an owl sitting on a tree next to us as we were cleaning the stables ready for Burmese and co. It's true Beatrix Potter country.

Henry is outside, finishing off the stables with the boys at the moment as the horses arrive in two days, a lot earlier than planned, as the children are so excited. The girls are beside themselves with excitement for their arrival and have already worked out a rota for their care. Penny is playing with her toys with Agatha and Etta, and the older three girls are unpacking our books onto the built-in book shelves in our sitting room.

We've all been getting on so well, the move really seems to have brought us closer together. Even The MIL seems more relaxed. We let her have a wander this morning but she wasn't keen on being out for very long (far too cold for her). However, the farmhouse seems to have met with her approval. She's spent most of her time wrapped in a ball, on a rug next to the open fire in the dining room, purring and eyeing the dogs with her usual disapproving sapphire eyes on the rare occasion they dare to enter and disturb her.

We've met a few of the villagers too. Henry popped to the only shop in the village early yesterday morning to arrange to have newspapers delivered. He came back an hour later with his arms filled with twelve fresh eggs, two farmhouse loaves of bread still warm from the oven, a homemade cake and some local smoked bacon wrapped in brown paper.

'Where did this come from?' I asked as he placed it all on the kitchen work top.

'Would you believe it! I went in to order the papers and Andrew, the owner, leaned across the counter and shook my hand then gifted us this lot. A "settling in present" he said. I did try to pay for it but he wouldn't hear of it.'

'That's unbelievable. What a lovely man.'

'Isn't it just. He's a true gent, that's for sure.'

That same day we were all in the playroom; Henry was putting up some shelves and the children and I were arranging their craft station when a buzzer started ringing loudly through the house. The noise caused us all to stop in our tracks and look at each other. It took a moment to register what it was.

'Ah, it's the gate. There must be someone here,' Henry said.

'I wonder who it is,' I said as we walked over to the intercom and looked at our CCTV screen.

I could see two men in matching hunting jackets. The blonde man was very tanned and chubby and the other had jet-black hair, a muscular build, and was wearing a pair of glasses. They stood next to each other, leaning on an Audi Q7.

Henry pushed the intercom. 'Hello, can I help you?'

The blonde man lent forward and smiled at the intercom. 'Hiya. I'm Quinn. My husband Richard and I live at Primrose Rise, the stone thatched cottage by the bridge. We heard from Sally in the pub that you moved in so we thought we would come and say hi and give a house-warming present.'

'Oh, that's very kind of you. Come on up and have a drink with us if you have the time?'

'We would love that. See you in a mo.'

As we sat round our table with coffee and shared the Victoria sponge cake that Andrew, the kind man from the village shop had given us, we soon learned more about Richard, Quinn and the village we had just made home. Richard was a businessman like Henry, very strong-minded and they bonded over similar life experiences while Quinn and I got along straight away. I love his quick wit as much as he enjoys my sarcasm.

They gave us the lowdown on who's who in the village and

all about themselves. Quinn owns an art gallery, one we've passed in the next village each time we've visited, where he makes pottery and sculptures for a living. Richard works away three days a week 'in the big smoke' and holds an extremely high position with a big financial company. They're such good people and they adored our children. The feeling was mutual; even Penny, who's at an age where she's wary of new people, gave them both a kiss on the cheek as they left. We've arranged for them to come for supper next weekend and they left us a beautiful wicker hamper lined with Fortnum & Mason tea towels and bursting with artisan treats.

'They're just brilliant. I think we'll become close friends with them, don't you?' I said as I watched their shiny grey Audi disappear down our drive.

'Aren't they just? Everyone we've met so far has confirmed this move was the right decision.'

'Mum! Edward is trying to stab Charles with a fork! MUM!' Nora urgently bellowed.

'Edward, PUT THE FORK DOWN. DON'T YOU DARE STAB YOUR BROTHER!'

'I'll go. Some things don't seem to change though,' said Henry smiling as he jogged off down the hall to find Edward.

Evening

Glad we decided to stay home this evening. I'm currently lounging in my favourite ancient flannel PJs and cashmere socks with a hot coffee and a box of Lindt chocolates, admiring our new day/kitchen room while I wait for Henry to finish setting up his telescope so we can watch a film afterwards. The wood burner's roaring and both dogs are sprawled out by my feet. Outside is completely black. I've never known such darkness; apart from the garden and pond lights that are darted around the grounds, you can't see in front of your nose yet I don't even feel the need to close the curtains. There's no one or nothing (apart from an abundance of wildlife, including a family of bats that keep swooping around our kitchen window) for miles around.

The younger children are asleep after a few really unsettled nights (which we expected, being in a new house) but today they went to bed after their story, happy and in good spirits. Even Penny hasn't woken up as of yet and she usually needs re-settling constantly. Martha, Margot and Nora are in their new rooms reading. We've noticed such a change in them. The older girls having their own rooms has made a difference to them all, the arguing has decreased dramatically.

My handsome husband has just come and got comfy next to me so we're going to see the New Year in together by watching a film, drinking coffee and eating carrot cake. We know how to party!

JANUARY

Wednesday 2nd January

11 a.m.

Tara is expecting at least eight puppies! She's just had a check-up and scan today at our new vet. We're going to start getting her whelping box made and order birth supplies this week so we are well prepared. Henry's downstairs office is off our day room and will be our puppy room because she needs her own space. It has a flagstone floor too which means I can keep it clean. Henry's not too chuffed about being evicted from his man cave but he'll just have to work from the dining room table like I do until the pups are old enough to go to a puppy playpen in the stables.

3 p.m.

Margot just came into the kitchen and handed me Henry's phone (one downside of country living — crap phone signal.) It was Jean; she sounded a bit fed up.

'Hello, chick, I've been trying to ring you for ages. Finally got through to Henry. Anyway, just to let you know we've got them all loaded. That horse of yours is a bugger to get on. Cor, did he give me a time of it! Reared, spooked, kicked out, the handsome old devil! Anyway, we're en route and will be with you in the next half an hour. I hope the box fits through the gates. Can you get your boots on and walk down to the end of the road in the next twenty minutes in case I can't fit through and I can't get you on the phone?'

'Yes, shall do. Sorry you've had problems that end.'

'No bother. I've dealt with worse over the years; not much worse mind!' she replied with a chuckle.

I went into the hallway to the bottom of the stairs and called up. 'That was Jean, everyone! Burmese and the ponies will be here anytime so can we all get our boots on and make sure the dogs are in? We need to walk down the drive to meet them.'

It's funny how fast children can get coats and wellies on when they want to. Within ten minutes we were all walking down our drive, Penny in her purple snowsuit, snuggled in her buggy being pushed by Martha, and Henry carrying Charles who, despite his excitement, was true to form and refused to stand on the buggy board.

Jean's big, old, bright red wagon with a blue painted sign in the front that read 'HORSES' soon came into sight. Everyone, including Henry and I, started waving and dancing around like idiots. Jean nodded her head and smiled and Jacki, her groom, waved. The lorry drew to a standstill and Jean wound down her window and leaned out.

'Hello, everyone. I won't get the old girl up that drive so we'll have to unload here and walk them up.'

'Okay, that's fine. I thought we may have to,' I replied. Henry, who has never been very comfortable around horses, especially Burmese who is a horse that never misses an opportunity to be given the chance, quickly announced that he had no intention of being anywhere near the horses during unloading.

'Right, I'll walk back up to the house with the kids and we'll come back out when the horses are all safely at the stables.'

His decision wasn't a popular one with the children.

'Owwwhhhh, Daaaddd! We don't want to go to the house!' they all moaned.

'Come on! The sooner we go, the sooner the ponies will be unloaded and you can see them,' Henry said as he started to walk back up the drive. They all reluctantly followed, knowing there was little point arguing with him.

'What order are they loaded, Jean?' I asked.

'Your boy is first to come out, Alice,' Jean's groom answered as she ventured up the ramp.

'Best leave him to Alice, Jacki, she's used to his unique ways,' Jean warned

'Right-O.' Jacki didn't need much convincing.

Burmese was sweating. His always glossy, black coat was

shining and steaming and he was watching me with wide eyes and looking extremely agitated. This was further confirmed by his angry head thrashing and his thunderous feet stomping. I had seen his routine many times before so I wasn't overly worried. He'd never been a good traveller and, although a hot head, wasn't an unkind horse. He was never one to take it out on his handler; he just had his own mind and needed careful handling when he was in this frame of mind.

I decided to stop putting off the inevitable and so opened the divider and replaced his head collar with a bridle and bit and then swapped his lead rope for a lunge rein in order to give him some space if he blew up completely, which he had been known to do after a stressful journey. After a quick pat and a Polo from my pocket and a click of my tongue, I began to lead him off the box.

As I predicted, he attempted to rush out of the box in a panic. Thankfully, with a few calm words, he came back to me and clambered off the wagon, his hooves clattering. He visibly relaxed once he was out but then began calling to his friends who were still patiently waiting in the lorry. Whilst Roman was unloaded by Jacki, I let Burmese have his head and graze on the grass border. He visibly relaxed within minutes. We then made our way up the long driveway and, apart from the odd spook at the shadows from our driveway lights, he was an angel. We were soon joined by Star and Tinker. Jean was keen to get back on the road so said her goodbyes and set off.

The children and I took off the ponies' travel boots and

gave them a small feed, after which they'd all cooled down and stopped sweating so I rugged them up. Star has problems with allergies, meaning she has to live outside in the fresh air. Star and Tinker were put together in our paddock near the house with a field shelter while Roman and Burmese were put into adjacent stables. Both of them dropped to their knees and rolled in their fresh, deep bed of shavings before getting back on their feet.

We left them happily munching their haynets that the girls had filled and soaked this morning. As the kids and I walked back around to the kitchen patio door (which has become our main entrance in and out of the farmhouse), we passed the ponies who were illuminated by the pond lights. They could be seen happily grazing.

The children ran ahead while I hung back for a moment to take it all in, letting my surroundings sink in. We lived in the countryside in a farmhouse with horses. We had actually done it!

Sunday 10th January

1 p.m.

Tinker escaped today. He was by the feed room with his head buried in a bag of chaff when Henry happened to clock him out of his office window. The little shit had the electric fencing down again. It took us the best part of an hour, two packets of organic, washed baby carrots that were meant for our supper this evening and an enormous amount of sprinting, combined with some pretty wild hand gestures to get hold of him. He is seriously fast for a fat little fucker. We've decided to move him into the large field with Burmese which is really secure and to have the rail round the pony paddock repaired properly ASAP.

I then spent the rest of the morning bribing the little people with endless packets of Skips and mint Club bars so I could help Henry build Tara's whelping box. Three hours of pure hell, holding pieces of wood together 'really still' while being barked at to pass various screwdrivers.

I'm about sick of Henry already today so I'm going to escape to the shops and take as few children with me as possible. That will teach him, the shouty bloody bastard. Admittedly I did lose concentration for a moment or two when an advert for Magic Mike came on the television and I dropped his electric screwdriver on his foot twice. Although I'm inclined to say I'm a believer in karma so therefore possibly the universe may well have dished out what was deserving to him for calling me idiotic for not knowing what a Phillips screwdriver was and shouting, 'Wake the fuck up!' after the first unfortunate tool-dropping incident.

Evening

Epic tantrum from Margot this afternoon, all over her choice of outfit. If you remember, I planned to escape to the shops and leave Henry in the shit to teach him a lesson and so

I'd asked who wanted to come to Waitrose with me, playing it down, we weren't buying treats and they would have to help me pack it all. Only Edward and Margot said yes to coming (result!) so I sent them both upstairs to have a quick wash and get some 'suitable clothes on'.

Edward came back down first, wearing a pair of brown cord trousers and an ancient lambswool jumper — perfect winter, pop-to-the shops wear. He was closely followed by Margot who was one hundred percent not wearing perfect pop-to-the-shops wear. Instead she had gone down the route of perfect pop to the strip club wear.

She looked ridiculous. In she swaggered, wiggling her bum in a skin-tight pair of white hot pants over the top of a pair of red, opaque tights and a red, skin-tight belly top with a white 'SELFIE' slogan printed across the front.

'What on *earth* are you wearing? You aren't coming out with me dressed like that, Margot,' I said, staring at her hot pants and trying to work out where they'd come from.

'I am!' came the defiant reply.

I shook my head at her. 'You are not! Henry, come here. Look at what this child is wearing!' I shouted, sensing reinforcements were going to be needed.

'That's not even her top and shorts, Mum. They're Etta's, age FIVE!' Martha said while laughing and smirking at Margot.

'Margot, go and take it off please and put something warm on. It's freezing. We're going to the supermarket. You can't wear age five shorts to Waitrose, darling.'

97

'I knew you would do this!' Margot screamed at me.

'Do what? Honestly, Margot, they're not suitable for you to wear out at all really. They're not even yours. Please just go and put something else on. What about those nice jeans and that lovely roll neck you got for Christmas?' I asked as calmly as possible, wondering where Henry was hiding.

'YOU ARE CLOTHES SHAMING ME! People *do* wear clothes like this in winter! What about the lady we saw in the rain, waiting for a taxi? That was in winter and she was wearing a bikini and a kaftan!'

'That was outside Cape Verde airport. She wasn't in a supermarket in England buying her weekly shop.' I tried not to laugh.

'Well, Kourtney Kardashian wears hot pants and boob tubes and she's a mum,' she replied as she folded her arms and stared at me.

'Yes, you're right. She *is* a mum but I'm *your* mum and so you have two choices — either get dressed or don't come. Either way, I'm leaving in five minutes.'

She disappeared back upstairs and soon waltzed back into the kitchen. I was now speechless. Her look had gone from *Pretty Woman* to the rapper Notorious B.I.G. Not only did she have exactly the same outfit on but had now upgraded it and was now also sporting a velvet choker, a black flat cap, a pair of black, oversized sunglasses that she bought at a Turkish market last summer and her very glamorous, very OTT, floor-length, faux fur coat that Beryl and Clive had given her for Christmas.

'Right, that's it! You can stay here, young lady. You look ridiculous,' I shouted, heading for the door, Edward trailing behind me with a stack of bags for life piled high in his arms.

Not one to give in easily, Margot shouted back at me, 'I've had enough of you people! How dare you! I have a right to free choice! I know my human rights. Someone, call me an Uber. You've gone too far this time! I'm leaving this stupid, green place!'

Before I could respond, she turned on her heels and stormed out of the patio, slamming the door behind her, so hard the frame wobbled.

I looked out of the window and could see her stomping off towards the horse paddock. Henry resurfaced, joining me at the window, scratching his head and looking puzzled as we both looked on at Margot who was now attempting to climb over the paddock gate; easier said than done wearing a fully lined, full-length, faux fur coat that probably weighs more than you do and being nuzzled by three greedy ponies the other side of the fence who think you may have come bearing Polos.

'What on earth is she wearing?' Henry asked, laughing while watching her march towards the ponies' field shelter.

'Oh don't ask,' I said.

'You and Edward go, darling. I'll call her in when she calms down,' Henry said, still laughing and shaking his head.

Waitrose was quite a trek from the house but we found it easily and stocked up for the week. On our return, Edward and I hadn't even got out of the car before the dogs were circling us, full of excitement, then Henry waved from the front door, a grin on his face. He walked over to the car and opened my door.

'I'll get this lot. You go and have a coffee. Margot won't come in. It's turned into a bit of a sitting protest. She's in the field shelter, refusing to move; claims she will not be coming out of the paddock until she receives a full apology in writing from you and if she doesn't get one, she will be contacting 'the powers that be'. I've just sent Martha out to ask her if she wants a hot chocolate.'

In this house Nora puts away the shopping; she's a natural organiser and loves doing the task and it's well worth the £5 fee that she 'charges' for her efforts so, while she got on with emptying the bags, Henry was explaining to Charles and Etta why we couldn't really have a reindeer even though 'yes, admittedly we do now have the land.'

I had made a start to peeling some potatoes for supper when I caught sight of Margot aka Kourtney K (albeit slightly less paparazzi ready after staging a three-hour sitting protest in the middle of a mud field) emerging from the field shelter and stomping towards the farmhouse. She stropped through the door, lifted her sunglasses, and rested them on the top of her head.

'Right! I'm willing to make a deal with you people. If you stop being so overbearing, I'm willing to stay on a trial basis and see how things go.' she said in a stern voice.

It took all my strength not to laugh. Agatha, who had been watching the *Antz* movie on the sofa with Penny, looked over and called out to her, 'Oh, hello, Margot. I thought you were moving to Dubai?' then continued to question her. 'Have you gone and come back? That was fast. Can I borrow your coat so I can play Narnia?'

Margot rolled her eyes and ignored her. Nora, who had been putting away all the cereals and jars in the pantry, walked back into the kitchen, took one look at Margot, pulled a wide-eyed, amused expression, and said, 'Margot, why are you dressed like Grandma Beryl? You look mental. No wonder Mum wouldn't let you go with her, you weirdo.'

That pushed Margot over the edge. She huffed, she puffed, then stormed upstairs, screeching all the way about 'idiot people' and how she wished she was 'Tracy Beaker and lived in a children's home.' She stomped downstairs a short while after and ate her steak pie and mashed potato, refusing to join in any conversations, dumped her plate on the side then disappeared back upstairs to watch *Dance Moms*.

I called up to her an hour or so later and asked if she wanted some jam roly-poly and custard. She shouted a sulky 'Yes, not the end bit though,' then sauntered down in her unicorn onesie like nothing had happened. Thank goodness no one mentioned anything more about it.

Tomorrow is the children's first day at their new school. I hope they all get on okay. I've been reminding them all they must stick together and make sure each other are okay because, regardless of the little squabbles they have at home, they're family and they must look out for one another, especially at playtime and lunch. I'm so glad they all have each other; it would be even worse if they had to go it alone.

Monday 11th January

11 a.m.

They all looked so smart before school today. The girls had their hair French braided. Edward, with his blonde hair freshly cut, swaggered in his royal blue wool duffel and new lace-up brogues. (Henry said he looked like a City trader and possibly a bit too extra for his first day at a village infant school but he didn't, he looked lovely.) He made my heart melt when he strode over to the car door and held it open for all his sisters then carried all their book bags.

I was eyeballed by the parents as we walked through the playground, but not in an unkind way. A few people said, 'Good morning,' which was nice. We were met in reception by Mr Plait, the head teacher, who was in his usual upbeat mood.

'Morning children, Mrs Babylady. How are we all? You all look so smart! Now, don't be nervous children, I've chosen you all a lovely new class buddy to help you get used to the school and find your way and I'll make sure you can all sit next to each other at lunch. How does that sound?'

It was smiles and grins all round and I watched five of my little babies happily skip off with their school teachers, who had appeared out of the staff room, to start their first day in their new school.

I stayed behind to pay their dinner money for the term. As I was filling in the menu choices for the next week, two women came into reception. The taller woman had a blunt, brown bob and a strong jaw line and was wearing a white blouse with a PTA badge pinned to it. The other lady had sweaty blonde hair that was scraped back, exposing her red-flushed face. At a guess I would say she'd either power walked or cycled to school as she was wearing sports leggings and a quite unforgiving gym top and was breathing heavily while guzzling from her water bottle and glancing at the Fitbit around her wrist.

'You must be the newbie?' said the woman with the PTA badge. I noticed she was frowning at my watch as I signed the last lunch menu form.

'Yes. Hello, I'm Alice,' I said brightly, smiling at them both.

'Hello, I'm Clair. Lovely to meet you. I have a son in your daughter's class. Did they all go in okay?' asked the lady in the sportswear.

'Thank you, yes. They were all a little apprehensive but they have each other at least,' I replied, still smiling.

'Yes, you've got a lot of them, haven't you? How many is it? Six? Or have you lost count? You know what causes that, don't you?' spat the woman with the bob and the PTA badge which I was now beginning to think could stand for Petty Twattish Army.

'Amanda, the raffle prizes are in the hall ready for you,'

said the receptionist as she gathered up my forms then turned and shook her head, giving me a kind smile.

The badge woman had riled me so I turned back to her still smiling, but with my eyes fixed sternly on hers. 'I have eight children, not six, and I am well aware what's causing them, thank you. You see, it's my view that I'm doing the world a favour, hopefully helping to balance the planet-moron to decent human being ratio but it seems evident that I'm fighting a losing battle. Anyway, I shan't keep you.'

Clair, who had been taking another swig of her water, coughed and spluttered.

'Right, come along, Clair. We have a raffle to arrange. Sorry, what was your name again? Never mind. Anyway, we have to run. I have very important official PTA duties,' said a flustered Amanda, clearly not used to anyone challenging her behaviour.

'Bye, Alice, nice to meet you,' called Clair as she followed Amanda.

I turned back to the reception window. 'Mrs Jackson, how does one go about signing up to the PTA?'

'Well, umm, you can just tell me and then, well, you've joined really although Amanda has taken the position to run things unofficially so to speak, but not officially, and please call me Phillipa.'

'I would like to join then please, Phillipa.'

'Excellent! I will let all the members know and will email you a meeting schedule,' she replied rather too enthusiastically.

'Oh, please do and please also pass the message on to the current members that I'm very much looking forward to working with them and that I fully intend to be VERY involved,' I replied.

'It will be my pleasure to do so,' Phillipa said with a smirk.

'Oh, one other thing. Will I get a badge?' This was too much for Phillipa and one of the teaching assistants who was filling in an accident book. They both looked at me then each other and burst out laughing.

Phillipa tried to gain composure by holding her nose and said, 'Sorry, I'm afraid not. The school doesn't supply badges. However, Amanda may be able to point you in the right direction as to where she had hers made.' More laughter from the office.

'Oh right, well, I'm not sure I would go as far as commissioning one myself. Maybe Amanda would consider letting me wear hers from time to time instead,' I said, straight-faced.

'Oh gosh, I'm leaving now before I have an accident and have to change my Tena Lady!' said the teaching assistant through snorts of laughter as she walked past me and gave me a wink, passing Mr Plait, who gave her a confused look.

'All settled and happy. I'll give you a call at lunch to update you but rest assured they're in good hands!' he said, still beaming at me.

'Thank you, that's good to know.'

'Mr Plait? Mrs Babylady is joining the PTA! Isn't that great news?' said Philippa.

'EXCELLENT. I am delighted. Also, I meant to ask you. Haven't you got a swimming pool up at your place?'

'We have but it needs a bit of work before it's useable,' I replied, not quite cottoning on.

'EXCELLENT. It would be wonderful for the children to be able to have lessons there! Let's chat at the next PTA about it?'

'Um, okay then,' I said while thinking what children did he mean; hopefully mine?

So I am now a PTA wanker. Henry came into his office a moment ago, frowning down at Penny pulling apart his Post-It notes and dotting them around the floor as I checked out a WHSmith order, having decided I needed some new note books, a Filofax and posh pen.

'What's wrong with the Filofax you have?'

'Nothing, but that's a work one. I need a school and PTA one.'

When he had stopped howling with laughter, he said, 'PTA? You said you would never be involved with the PTA!'

'Well, things change. I want to make friends here and be involved with the children's school,' I replied with a smile on my face.

'God help them!' he said, shaking his head and still laughing.

4 p.m.

Just picked the children up from school. They LOVED it.

Feel so relieved. All of them have various party and supper invitations, which has really pleased them. The parents have been so welcoming, apart from Amanda, that is. She marched up to me when I was waiting at the collection area and wasted no time in marking her territory.

'I need to speak to you. It's come to my attention that you are intending to join my PTA?' she snarled at me.

'Your PTA? I thought it was a school PTA? But, yes, I will be attending the next meeting and intend to be involved.'

'Well, do not get ahead of yourself. There is not much for you to do and I run things around here,' she snorted.

'I can always find something,' I said, grinning at her as she frowned and turned on her heel.

'She's so bloody rude,' came a remark from a well-dressed woman standing next to me. 'Glad I caught you,' she continued. 'I'm Lara. I live opposite the pub in the pink house. Don't take any notice of Amanda. She's cross because you got Puddle-Duck Farm, wanted it for herself you see but they couldn't get a mortgage so it's a case of sour grapes. She isn't at all nice at the best of times. Anyway, as I said, I'm glad I caught you. Philippa in the office and I were talking and wondered if you liked reading? Some of us mums get together every other Thursday to have some lunch, a book club of sorts and we wondered if you wanted to join in?'

'Um, yes please. I love to read.'

'Lovely. Next Thursday then? Joyce is hosting next week. She lives in the stone house next to the duck pond with the old farm tools on the wall. Do you know the house I mean?'

'Yes, I've seen it, it's beautiful.'

'It is, isn't it? Well, I look forward to you coming along then! No doubt see you before though,' she said, smiling.

'I expect so. Thanks again for inviting me.'

'You are most welcome.'

So, I might make some new friends and at least I know why Amanda is so off with me.

Wednesday 12th January

Henry and I have decided to get some pigs. Henry wants to rear them for meat and to teach the children 'where food really comes from'. I've agreed so he lets us get them but I have no intention of actually eating them. We've just bought a second-hand pigsty on Gumtree and it's being delivered this weekend. I want to also get some more chickens and goats then start on the vegetable patch when the weather gets better. It's going to be like *The Darling Buds of May* here; just watch this space.

I'm going to be on my own with the kids for four nights next month and I'm a little bit worried about it so we've also been researching Mastiff dogs. We've found a breed that's bred to guard the homestead, especially farms. They're rare in this country but we've found a breeder who has some puppies so we're going to visit them later this week.

Henry, as you know, is desperate for another dog and,

having read all about these Mastiffs, I'm all for it. Although we live in a basically crime-free area, with Henry going away with work a few days a month, I would feel better having a dog to protect us all. Tara and Chubb, as lovely as they are, wouldn't save us from an intruder. I doubt they would even wake up, well, not unless the burglar came for the fridge. Everyone we've contacted has said these dogs are excellent with children but that they're very powerful so need a confident owner. We have a lot of large dog experience so I hope we'll be suitable for them and vice versa.

Evening

Henry's really fallen in love with the Mastiffs the more he reads and has spoken to various different breeders to make sure the one we are going to meet is reputable. He's just shown me some pictures of the pups left. Obviously completely gorgeous but older and a lot bigger than I expected; five and a half months and already around 45 kilos. They were both due to go to South Africa but the owners have had a change of circumstances so the dogs are available. We are going to see them tomorrow.

***

I've been having a bit of a Mum rant this evening after I found Martha's PE kit in her bag after I'd already asked her if she had any dark washing. I'm sure everyone in this house thinks we have a cleaning and cooking fairy who does everything for them. The problem is they do have one — me! I don't mind doing it all but I think they all forget I'm also holding down a job part-time from home and so picking up after themselves and making their own beds from time to time wouldn't go amiss. I may make a chores rota to put up on the wall for everyone to ignore.

Thursday 13th January

We now have four dogs. Yes, FOUR. We arrived at the breeder's house about eleven this morning and were introduced to two clumsy, adorable puppies who are at that awkward stage — all legs and humongous paws. It was love at first sight.

Although they're sisters, they're completely different, but equally endearing. One is so wide she is almost square; built like a tank, with rolls of fat. She is so confident and bolshy, came in like a whirlwind, demanding attention but, upon seeing the children, immediately stopped and calmed down and gently nudged Penny and Agatha with her nose before sitting by their feet for attention. We've called her Nancy.

Then her sister came in shyly and sat by my feet, shaking and rolled over submissively then quietly went and lay by her sister, rolling over onto her back to encourage the children to stroke her, where she stayed, still as a statue, eyes closed, until the children moved away from her. She is now called Daisy. As soon as I saw how gentle they both were with the children and how close they both were, I decided there was no way I was leaving without the two of them.

'Oh, Henry, aren't they lovely! Look, they're so bonded. It would be wicked to separate them. What do you think?' I asked him with a pleading look in my eyes.

'Two would be hard going but you have the knowledge. If you did want to take them both, I would be happy for them to go together,' said their breeder eagerly.

'I agree. We can't separate them. I'm taken with them both as well and it would be unfair to split them up, and I couldn't decide between them so yes, we will have them both,' said Henry who was sitting on the floor with Penny on his lap.

Half an hour later, we had parted with over £4,000 and had two new family members. We are going to have our work cut out. I know from experience that one puppy is hard work but these are two giant pups and will be a huge challenge. I have a feeling shit is about to get real but they will give me so much peace of mind when I'm alone on the farm with the children and they already are proving to be excellent friends and guardians to the children.

Evening

The children are in love with the pups and it's very much a mutual feeling. They follow the children round like lost sheep. Henry and I cannot believe how gentle they are. Chubb and Tara also like them, they all fell asleep together by the fire earlier. We've decided not to let them outside at the same time as Tara as they get very excited in the garden and we're worried they may barge into her and, given they weigh nearly as much as her, it's not something I'm willing to risk with her being pregnant.

We stopped on the way home at Pets at Home and picked up two XXXL dog crates for night-time, just while they're getting to grips with toilet training. They'd been kennelled at their breeders but they are now part of our family and will live in the house just like our other dogs do so I will be using the crates to house train them and when they get a little bit too excited in the daytime.

It's amazing that, despite not even being six months old, they have such a strong guard instinct. Our hay man came this evening and both stood between him and me and barked at him then just stood there watching him. Amazingly, as soon as I said 'Good girls,' to them and they saw me shake hands with him, they relaxed but stayed close by watching him, which is exactly how Henry and I hoped for them to be. They're not so brave with The MIL, one hiss from her sent them both squealing and darting to safety so she knows she has the upper hand and is taunting them constantly. It's all wasted efforts, however, as it seems they're quick learners and have given her a wide berth since, which is for the best really.

Friday 14th January

Morning

Daisy and Nancy are bringing so much fun into our lives. Both of them are so full of character, they're a pleasure to be around. Talk about really loving life! I'm watching them now, darting around the gardens chasing each other, not a care in the world. They've even got Chubb to act silly and play with them and he's not really one to get himself involved usually. They've also had no accidents since the first night so, before bed yesterday, I decided to let them stay in the hallway. Stupidly Henry and I thought they wouldn't attempt the stairs. I woke up the next morning to find Nancy sprawled out at the bottom of Etta's bed and Daisy star fishing on her back by Penny's cot, snoring heavily, but we couldn't complain as they hadn't caused any damage whatsoever. What superstars.

5 p.m.

I've just endured a traumatic life event. I can now state with utmost certainty that unless you've never been stuck inside an item of clothing — like completely can't-even-move-your-arms fucking stuck — you have never known real fear.

Despite Henry's un loyal mutterings of, 'You've been quite indulgent over Christmas, darling. You should have probably ordered a bigger size,' I will be forever grateful to him for cutting me free with a pair of nail scissors. And, for the record, the dress I was sent, and almost suffocated in, was (despite what the label stated) not a size 10, therefore River Island will be shortly receiving a very strongly worded email demanding a full apology and urging them to have a serious bloody look at their sizings before anyone else is humiliated like I've just been.

In all seriousness, there are some things you cannot un-see

or un-hear and your husband panting while telling you to 'hold your belly fat down and take a REALLY deep breath' so he can insert a pair of scissors to cut you free will haunt me forever. I also suspect Henry would list witnessing my wobbly bits bulge and strain like a tightly stringed pork joint while I had a 'claustrophobic-based panic attack' pretty high on his wish he could un-see list. How humiliating. Fucking River Island!

Thursday 20th January

Just popped in to see Quinn at his gallery. I told him about Amanda and the book club. He's invited himself along next week. I did say I wasn't sure he would be allowed to come on account of it being a woman's book club. His response was, 'Oh, don't be silly. I'm gay and we can go everywhere. I love a good Jilly Cooper... Rupert Campbell-Black, PPHHOOAARR,' and that's why we get on so well. He's so funny and has excellent taste.

Quinn also knows so much about fashion and interiors, he's promised to come around next week to help me rearrange my sitting room and start a mood board to decide what colour statement wall I should go for in Henry's office. Henry has said he doesn't want a statement wall but he does really, he just doesn't know it yet.

I also filled Quinn in on the River Island faulty sized clothes episode. He was furious for me and agreed that having a near-death experience and having to be cut out of a dress by my husband isn't on at all and suggested I tweet them. I don't have Twitter so he's going to use Richard's work Twitter account to send them a public rant because it has thousands more followers than his does and said that it will 'shit the sizeist bastards up.' I asked if Richard would mind us using his global, very-important-job account to send abuse to a high street store and he assured me Richard definitely wouldn't as long as we didn't use the C word like he did when he got a little too 'emotionally invested' when Peter Andre left Katie Price.

Friday 23rd January

1 p.m.

My new car came this morning! After Henry succeeded in convincing me that my coupé wasn't suitable for a mum of eight who lives in the country, I am now a Land Rover Discovery owner. Between the two 4x4s on the driveway and all my dependants of the two- and four-legged variety, I feel quite grown up. Going to my first PTA meeting now. Hoping I won't be the only one taking children with them. Surely I won't be, we are all mums, after all.

4 p.m.

I was the only one with children. I'm not counting a woman who had her twins with her because she also had an au pair who looked after them the whole time. I might get an au pair; not a young, hot one though like the woman at the meeting had. I wonder if there's an agency that supplies old, non-hot ones suitable for women under 30 with handsome husbands…

Anyway, thankfully my three non-au-pair-accompanied little people behaved themselves and no one seemed to care they were there, even when Penny shrieked at me for not letting her climb on a stack of boxes full of outdoor play equipment. I had, however, planned ahead and brought some diversions of the no-nutritional-value and electronic variety. About twenty minutes in, Penny, having missed her lunchtime nap, crashed out on a blue PE matt, holding a half-eaten Barney Bear cake bar in one hand and her beloved filthy rag — 'the Yanit' — in the other and Charles sat himself down on a wooden PE bench which had been left out after afternoon assembly and was engrossed in *Jurassic Park* on his iPad. Amanda, who, it turns out, is a bit of a judgemental cow as well as a twat who buys her own PTA badges, muttered to the woman next to her (knowing full well I could hear), 'Is that really suitable viewing? I mean, I know it's a PG but is it *really*?'

I resisted getting into it with her, on the basis you cannot educate pork. Agatha was her usual, larger than life self. She listened with interest and was the first to raise her hand when Amanda asked for volunteers to meet and greet parents at the upcoming book swap. She is such a people person (Agatha not Amanda). I think she will love pre-school when she and Edward start next week.

After the meeting, Mr Plait took the opportunity to ask me again about our swimming pool, saying how it upset him greatly that swimming lessons were not currently part of the school offerings as 'funds just didn't allow' and what a shame it was that the children were subsequently 'missing out on a vital life skill.'

I found myself saying Henry and I would make sure our pool was all up and running before the spring term and of course it could be inspected for safety and have the water tested each week and a professional report given to the school to cover them 'insurance wise' and 'don't be silly, Henry and I would be delighted to cover the costs.' What the actual fuck was I thinking? Henry will hit the roof when I tell him. He hates hordes of other people's children; not that he will be allowed to be in his own garden around them as he doesn't have all the valid police certificates that you need nowadays. Fuck's sake, I feel like I've really started something I will live to regret. I've turned into Florence, being all involved in the school, which is fine for her as she has a cleaner and no job and nothing else to do, but it's not fine for me as I don't have a cleaner and do have a job and shitloads to do. FMFL.

Saturday 24th January

Had all the girls over last night. It was an evening I had been really looking forward to. All my closest friends in one room for Fiona's birthday — Florence, with her Joanna Lumley voice; Sarah, my sensible (pre-wine) friend; Beth, a blonde bombshell, criminal law solicitor who's married to Henry's close friend, Marco (who is also drop dead gorgeous and a pilot); and the birthday girl, Fiona, head of a large PR firm and who is so sensible and controlled that she makes Sarah, who always has, without fail, completed her Christmas shopping by the first week in November, look wild.

Henry and Marco had agreed to look after the children for the evening (on the condition they were already in bed, asleep) and stay out of our way, which suited them as much as it did us. My husband and Marco like nothing more than to be holed up by an open fire, indulging in endless games of backgammon, eating fatty snacks and drinking gallons of coffee. An hour or so after everyone had arrived, it became apparent that the birthday girl wasn't her usual self. Before I had even got the mint and rosemary lamb shanks that I'd slow roasted with winter vegetables out of the range, Fiona, who despite not being a big drinker, had polished off several large glasses of white wine, had then proceeded to open one of the bottles of red on the table.

'What on earth has gotten into her? Since when does she drink red? Look at her glugging it back, that's an Aalto 2008 vintage! For fuck's sake what a waste. That was for us all to enjoy with our lamb!' exclaimed an outraged Florence as she watched, struggling to disguise the disgusted look on her face.

I glanced over at Fiona who was laughing loudly and pouring herself another glass of Florence's special red. She plonked herself down next to Beth and Sarah around the kitchen table, knocking over a water jug as she leant forward to refill her glass (again). Water landed all over my best tableware but thankfully the jug narrowly missed my large vase of winter peonies that Florence had picked up from our favourite florist from my old town.

As we ate our meal, we all looked on with matching confused expressions as our always serious and controlled friend, Fiona, became louder, funnier and more animated with every drink she had.

'The thing is, girls, I never used to worry about finding someone and settling down but here I am, 30 and alone and for what? Yes, I have a nice flat and a company car but I want a man and a child. My life is pointless; what do I have?'

'You've got your career, Fi! And you have your looks still. Anyway, what happened to the online dating? You never did tell us why you deleted your profile and what happened with that hunk?' ventured Beth.

'Yeah! He was a sort! I love a man with long hair,' slurred Florence who was also several large glasses of wine deep.

'Brad Pitt in *Troy*. Now that's a bit of me!' slurred Sarah.

'Corrr, yesssss!' we all agreed.

'Fuck it, I wasn't going to tell you all because it's so cringe but I will if you all swear it never leaves this room. You can never tell anyone else.' We all got very excited and nodded furiously at Fiona who got up and closed the door then summoned us over to my sofas on the other side of the open-plan kitchen. We all sat together like schoolgirls, bursting to hear why Fiona had deleted all her online dating profiles and why we've had to as good as sign a confidentiality contract for her to fill us in.

What followed was, without doubt, the most hilarious and humiliating incident I ever heard. I wish I could share Fiona's account involving Tinder, a Johnny Depp lookalike, and a train ride to Manchester. Sadly, it's not my story to tell and a promise is a promise so I cannot divulge further. This confession seemed to open the floodgates for all our inner worries and woes. Next up was Florence who, in anticipation of her turn, had already taken off her blouse ('just a last season's Marni, darlings, nothing special').

'As we are all being candid, darlings, I have no shame in admitting that the cellulite on my upper arms — look at it; gosh, it's revolting — has been concerning me so much I've been seriously considering not having my usual fortnight at Sandy Lane next month and you all know how much I value my winter break to Barbados. But at what cost? Can one really face the staff who have become friends and the guests when one has arms that look like a severely punched vagina? I just don't think I can...' She found it too much so stopped there and sobbed to a close.

Everyone, including me, was slightly too worse for wear to offer any real support or advice, agreed it was a real dilemma.

'Well, I'm off to Malia this summer, even with cellulite,' said Fiona.

'You're going where, darling?' questioned Florence who was buttoning her blouse back up.

'Malia! You know my cousin Tillie? She had an amazing

experience last summer out there and she reckons I would love the Malia vibe.' She ignored the snorts of laughter from us all and continued. 'I mean, you only live once. Tillie (who is barely out of school and, judging by her Instagram account, parties harder than the cast of *Geordie Shore*) has said she could put me up in her studio apartment above her work place, (an every-drink's-a-euro bar if my memory serves me correctly). I will probably just go for a fortnight. It's going to be brilliant. I'll get a killer tan, pull some fitties, drink cocktails and go out every night!'

I can't even write that without laughing. Unless you've met Fiona, you won't grasp just how funny that statement is but I'll try to explain. Fiona is the sensible friend, the Will McKenzie of the group, and while that isn't a bad thing (every friendship circle needs a Will, well, ours definitely does!) as, despite most of us being mums and us all having grown-up jobs, as I mentioned before we all do have a tendency to occasionally act like knobheads after a few glasses of wine. Fiona is the one who stops us in our tracks (usually, anyway, if she hasn't already fallen asleep) when we're in danger of getting too out of hand.

A good example of this is when Beth, before she met Mario, heard that her ex had a new girlfriend and so decided, in true female fashion, that she wanted him back. So, under the guidance of us (very pissed) best friends, she was all set to post a four-paragraph, open love letter to him via his social media pages.

It was going through its final edit (got to get those really descriptive words in there and Sarah, being a teacher, insisted on proofreading it all as 'you don't want to show yourself with poor grammar. It's penis with a small p not a capital one, Beth!') Then along comes Fiona who announces that she feels that Beth publicly posting to Tim (her ex) a message along the lines of, 'I miss your smooth pink balls that I shaved for you and your baby-soft but rock-hard penis (no idea) that makes me scream wildly with pleasure. I want you back in my vag and my heart,' was possibly a tad too much. Despite the rest of our protests for Fiona to pipe down and let Beth follow her own heart, Beth decided she maybe shouldn't post it after all.

Regrettably, during the confusion, Florence had somehow (purposely) managed to press 'post' on Beth's Facebook, resulting in the long post being visible on Beth's Facebook wall and she had also tagged in Tim, Tim's dad's plumbing business page ('just to pass the message on in case Tim didn't see it'), all his football and work mates and a woman who once made Beth a Christmas cake. (We aren't sure why she got involved; our only thoughts were that there may have been some unfortunate name-based confusion and she was mistaken for the new girlfriend.)

It didn't end that well although, credit where credit is due, Tim's dad took it extremely well despite his 3,787 online customers who visited his page ending up knowing all about his son's genitals and bedroom ability, and he sent Beth a really supportive inbox message:

Hi Beth,

Glad to see you're trying to get Tim back in your clutches... To level with you, I believe you're in with a good chance. As you know, Tim's bedroom is next to mine and Diane's and to be honest, we don't hear him and his new bit getting down to it half as much as we used to hear you two. It's a lot less frequent so I would go as far to say you may win him back on that basis. Fingers crossed. Hope I see you soon.

Vinnie

P.S. Say hi to your dad from me!

Beth went off the whole idea after that. Anyway, back to Fiona. What I'm trying to explain is that she's a bit of a goody two shoes (sorry, Fi) and, going by her past holiday history, she's really going to struggle if she goes to Malia. Fiona is much more suited to a weekend in Rome in a boutique hotel than two weeks in Malia, sweating her tits off in a non-air-conditioned, zero star-rated, shared studio. I really cannot imagine her liking 'the vibe' as much as she thinks she will. I mean, she's 30 now; does she really have any business downing pints of bright blue, vodka-based cocktails out of plastic fish bowls and eating three euro 'real English breakfasts'? On the other hand, it will be hilarious to see how she gets on. I may be proved wrong. Time will tell.

FEBRUARY

Sunday 1st February

Tara's puppies are due in two weeks. I cannot wait. She's so big now she looks like a waddling seal. She spends most of her time now asleep and the rest of it eating and she's loving every moment, mainly due to having free access to a puppy Complete biscuit for the higher protein content and mountains of cooked minced beef and chicken three times a day.

I have a PTA meeting later. Quinn is coming with me. He's been coming to all the meetings in the last few weeks. He started coming to 'even the numbers up' but he's really got himself involved and he hasn't let the fact he doesn't have any children hold him back. Things got a bit heated last week when we were asked our thoughts on how the money we will raise from the Valentine's Day disco should be spent.

Quinn was adamant he wanted it to go on an educational school trip and then told a disagreeing Amanda to 'shut the fuck up' when she dismissively shook her head and moaned how all the proceeds should go on new reading books for her son's class. Quinn then snapped back at her, shouting, 'All our children should benefit, not just *your* children! You need to think of all our children as well.'

Mr Plait looked a bit confused, probably due to the fact mentioned before that Quinn isn't actually a parent and has no connection to the school other than living in the village. However, Quinn has donated a very expensive vase from his gallery as a parents' assembly raffle prize plus he also always brings excellent biscuits and has bonded with Mr Plait, who he now smugly calls Robert, over their shared love of border terriers. So 'Robert dear' now backs and agrees with Quinn regardless.

'I can see Quinn's point of view Amanda, and I have to agree, I would also want the proceeds to benefit my child too, not just a select few,' said Mr Plait.

'Thanks Rob, hun,' said a nodding Quinn, throwing Amanda a superior grin.

Amanda tutted and rolled her eyes and sarcastically replied 'Quinn doesn't even have a child here so he doesn't get a vote!'

A few other mums nodded and then muttered comments like 'Yes, he shouldn't even *be* here, let alone have a vote', which was promptly nipped in the bud by Mr Plait.

'I am the head teacher, Mrs Eccle, and I say who gets to vote. Quinn and his husband have been very supportive of our school and are a very important part of this PTA board and so they *do* have a vote. Anyone who has an objection to that is free not to continue volunteering,' he said with a slightly raised voice.

Silence, came the stern reply and everyone pretended to look at their phones. We then moved on to the Valentine's Day disco.

I explained I wouldn't be able to help on the actual evening as Tara would be close to her due date but have agreed to make love tokens (little goody bags) and supply all the drinks and cups. I would never admit it to Florence or Henry but I'm quite enjoying the PTA, though not as much as Quinn obviously! I've always liked organising things and it feels good to give something back to the school that has been so welcoming to my children. Between being on the PTA and the book club I've made a few new mummy friends, which also is a major bonus.

Thursday 5th February

We are snowed in! Our garden looks like something out of Narnia. The school is closed so we've had a cosy day. Looking after animals in this weather is hard work though. Henry occupied the little ones who, dressed in ski suits and gloves, were happily playing in the snow. Daisy and Nancy ran riot, cavorting in it and flicking it with their noses, while Chubb, who wasn't so keen, opted, like Tara, to do his business as fast as possible and return to the warmth of the farmhouse.

I mucked out the stables while Agatha and Nora filled

haynets for Burmese and Roman, then piled three wheelbarrows high with hay and made the hard journey through the thick white blanket to the other side of the garden to the field gate and into the paddock, where they chucked it in high piles where the ponies would be sheltered from the elements by the thick trees.

Martha's job was to break the ice on the water troughs in the paddocks and refill them. Meanwhile Edward braved the deep snow and, with the help of Nora, piled our five bird tables with seed and hung fat balls. With Martha now playing with Charles and Penny, Henry waded through the drifts which had settled heavily around the pond to distribute duck food and bread to our resident ducks and swans. One of my last jobs was to check the ponies' heavyweight rugs and re-secure their neck covers.

Margot busied herself in each of the two field shelters by removing droppings from the rubber matting and emptying four bags of dust-free bedding into each one so the ponies will have some extra comfort should they choose to shelter from the cold and the next bout of snow showers, which the weather report claimed were soon heading our way.

My final job was to make four warm buckets of soaked Speedi-Beet and Keyflow. (Horses and ponies sometimes don't drink enough in the cold weather so soaked feed is a good way to make sure they're hydrated.) With the horses all fed, warm and happy, we all piled back into the farmhouse, tugged off our boots and wet, mud-covered clothes and dived into warm baths.

We decided it was a day for comfort, which meant lounging around in onesies eating heaps of beef stew from the slow cooker with crusty bread and watching films together with the fires crackling away. At supper time the snow started to fall again and we all stood watching the big flakes float past the patio doors of the day room. Our garden looked like a Christmas card and the children, who find any event out of the ordinary thrilling, bounced around while chanting, 'Yes! It's snowing so no school for us again tomorrow. Yay!'

Friday 6th February

Today was much like yesterday but with even more snow so no school again. The kids have been so hyperactive and had to be told countless times that the kitchen was not a place to practice judo and how I didn't care if 'Kevin did it all day in *Home Alone*, removing your mattresses from your beds and sliding down the staircase was never acceptable.'

Beryl and Clive are supposed to be coming for lunch on Sunday but I doubt they'll be coming now with all this snow.

Saturday 7th February

Still snowed in. Henry rang his parents to pre-warn them how bad the roads are here but they both seem adamant they'll be here as planned tomorrow. Henry told me his dad is planning on driving here in his 'dog car' which is an ancient Land Rover Defender that he used to drive his Cocker Spaniels around in before they passed away. Although it's perfect for this weather, I'm sure Beryl won't be happy. After all, 'one doesn't travel in a battered old farm truck that smells like wet dog and mud, what will the neighbours think!' I bet she kicks off and they end up coming in the E class.

Sunday 8th February

10 a.m.

Clive has just texted Henry:

Your bloody mother. She's refusing to come in the Land Rover!!! Having hysterics over the stains on the seats. Claims she also saw a flea which is just bollocks, it was a speck of dirt. I refuse to drive the Mercedes in this weather! Will either be coming in the truck or will have to cancel. About to put forward the idea of covering the seats with a picnic blanket.

I hope she refuses. I cannot be arsed to cook a roast today.

10:21 a.m.

They're on their way. Henry just got another text:

En route! Had to agree to buy a new Burberry blanket to replace the one she is now sitting on and a new bath towel to replace the one she has covering the footwell. See you around 1 p.m. We've overnight bags with us in case roads are bad and we have to stay.

Overnight bags... OH, FUCK OFF! Please, God, no. I'd better start peeling potatoes and get the lamb in. Bang goes my lazy afternoon reading the newspapers and eating cheese on toast while letting the kids run riot. I suppose I'd better get us all dressed as well. FMFL.

8 p.m.

We actually had a really good day. Clive and Beryl arrived about 2 p.m. They came clutching six bottles of Clive's homemade wine which, although delicious, gets you super pissed super quickly. Beryl got so blotto she didn't even moan about the lamb being overdone.

The children, perhaps sensing the laidback atmosphere, took full advantage of the relaxed situation and, after scoffing several helpings of lamb, Yorkshire pudding, roast vegetables and potatoes oozing in mint sauce, they disappeared, each clutching a bowl of apple pie and custard to camp out in front of the sitting room television where they stayed for hours, apart from regularly coming back for more and more bags of crisps and cake bars.

Henry only had one glass of wine so I could enjoy quite a few more without worrying about the kids. Beryl isn't that bad after a few drinks and so, after all of us deciding we did quite enjoy each other's company, Clive offered to pay for us all to go away for Easter to stay in a holiday house in Cornwall. How kind is that?

Henry kept trying to put us off booking it, pleading with us to 'have a sleep on it first' and saying over and over how we shouldn't 'act on it just yet'. Beryl, however, told Henry to be quiet and as he wasn't doing anything, he could refill her glass. Then, while Henry was occupied, she made Clive go onto holidaylettings.com to find a fancy cottage by the beach in Padstow that accepts dogs. She instructed him to 'whip out the Gold card' and they booked and paid in full.

So, we have a lovely family holiday to look forward to. Beryl and Clive are staying the night but they have to leave by nine as Clive has golf in the afternoon.

Going to sleep now as I have a busy day myself in the morning and Henry keeps saying how annoying I am when I'm drunk. The school is open in the morning but Henry's agreed to do the school run. I will still have to get up with Penny and help get the kids dressed and ready as he doesn't do the 'girly hair stuff'.

Monday 9th February

1 p.m.

Oh my fucking God. I feel awful. I wasn't feeling too bad when I woke up. After waving off the in-laws, I fed the animals and then started the daily mad rush to get everyone fed, dressed and ready but, as soon as I sat down at the table after Henry returned from his second trip to the school (dropping off Agatha and Charles at pre-school), I was hit with a headache that was so bad it hurt to blink. Henry took great pleasure in giving me a rundown of yesterday evening's events.

'So, darling, are you looking forward to our Easter break?'

'Pardon?' I was feeding Penny a yoghurt in one hand and holding my forehead with the other.

'Our little family holiday you agreed to go on with my mum and dad to Cornwall; end of April Easter week?' he replied with a smirk. He can be a right smug fucker sometimes.

'Yes, I am actually. I'm looking forward to it,' I lied. Oh why the fucking hell did I agree to a week in Cornwall with Beryl and Clive? What on earth was I thinking?

'Yes! I imagined you would be. Aren't we lucky? A whole week down in Cornwall with all the children and all four of the dogs and my parents. Luckily the puppies will be at their new homes by then. If not, you would've had to cancel which would have been impossible as it's been paid in full so instead we have a fun holiday to look forward to. Excellent!' Henry said, still smirking at me. He is one sarcastic knobhead.

Not wanting him to get any more pleasure from the current situation and because it hurt my head to speak and I needed hangover comfort food, I replied with a simple, 'Yes, we are very lucky. Do you want a bacon sandwich, darling?' I smiled through gritted teeth.

Wednesday 11th February

I'm only just feeling normal again! I must be getting old; a few years ago I could cure a hangover with a bacon sandwich and a litre of Tropicana and a lie down. Now it takes two days, two early nights, a multi-pack of Wotsits, six Kit Kats, lots of bacon sandwiches and more than one serious pep talk to remind myself to 'pull yourself together, you will get through this, just keep strong.'

There is a real buzz of excitement in the farmhouse as Tara's puppies could come any day. This afternoon Henry moved his desk out of his office and into our dining room and mission puppy room went underway. The children, who are set to burst at the thought of puppies, all lent a hand and together we cleaned the floor. Henry put the whelping box and pig rails into place. Henry's made the birth box from wood and the pig rails are placed around its perimeter to prevent the puppies being laid on by their mum.

Martha helped me line the bottom with non-slip, waterproof sheets and old towels. For hygiene I'll throw all the bedding away after the birth then replace it with washable vet bedding. Then we set up a little station with all the things I may need during the birth — sterile gloves, an aspirator, scissors and about a million other things. Lastly, we moved in a comfy chair and a lamp from the sitting room. I hope the birth is straightforward and goes well.

Thursday 12th February

12 p.m.

Henry is going ape. It seems the fully heated, fully working swimming pool is in fact fucked. We've had some gardeners getting all the grounds tidy and, before we get someone in to re-pave around the pool and the patio, Henry called out a swimming pool company to service it, get the water chemical levels right and set it up so it heats up and can be used. Well, that was the plan. The outcome was slightly different. The man came and, after disappearing into the control room, he re-emerged tutting and shaking his head.

'This pool heater will never heat the water volume it holds, especially in the winter months.'

'So it won't be usable in the winter, you mean, but okay in the summer months?' said Henry hopefully.

'Cor, you would be lucky for it to be warm enough to swim in a few days a year, given how it is at the moment!'

'Right, so what are our options?' replied Henry as a frown formed across his forehead at the thought of having to fork out more money.

'Well, you have two options. The first, the one I would recommend, an air-source heat pump.'

'And the second?' I asked, seeing Henry's face,

'Get yourself a wet suit!' chuckled the pool man.

'And there're no other options?' said Henry.

'Not unless you fill it in, no. It will be unusable until a new heat pump is put in.'

'And how much would one of those be, supplied and fitted?' Henry said, rolling his eyes.

Paul the pool man sucked his teeth. 'It won't be cheap, Mr Babylady. It's a big pool you have here. All in, you're looking at, fully fitted, seven and a half grand or thereabouts plus you need a decent pool cover.'

'No. No way! Thank you, Paul, but there's no way on earth I'm paying that. Seven and a half grand! Jesus Christ! For a pool heater! No way,' Henry said, shaking his head.

8 p.m.

Paul the pool man is coming next week to fit the heater. Once Henry calmed down, he saw sense. I think it was my threats to divorce him for being a tight arse and the children following him round pleading like a broken record, 'Please Daddy, please make our swimming pool hot. Please Daddy, we want to swim.' When he could take no more, he emailed and put an order in for a high-tech pool cover with safety alarms and the heat pump.

Friday 13th February

Henry's week just got worse. I've got him to drop the

children off at the PTA Valentine's school disco. What I haven't told him is that, when I said 'drop off', what I actually meant was drop them all off and stay for the whole two hours in order to supervise our children as per the rules. Which basically means he will have to watch our children, who will all pretend they don't know him, unless it's one of the hundred times they decide to take a minute away from being huddled in their age-and-gender-based scrums to shout over Justin Bieber to demand 'another quid for some crisps and a glow stick.'

Apart from when his money-providing services are required, he will stand redundant, wishing himself dead, awkwardly sipping an overpriced soft drink from a plastic cup (which, given we've supplied them, he will be paying for twice) whilst staring at his phone in order to avoid all potential eye contact with other parents and any consequent conversations that may arise.

Meanwhile Agatha, Charles and Penny are asleep so I'm going to curl up and watch *Location, Location, Location* and keep an eye on Tara in case she decides to have her babies. Judging by her current state, which is sprawled out snoring on the sofa, I very much doubt it. I could have taken the kids myself really but, well, I just didn't want to. I don't feel bad though. We all have to take one for the team sometimes and, unfortunately for Henry, today is his day.

Sunday 15th February

Nine perfect puppies have arrived. Five girls and four boys. Mum doing well. Too tired after being awake for over 24 hours so will fill you in when I've had a rest.

Monday 16th February

Friday seems so long ago, it must be all the sleep I've missed. Henry and the kids got back after the disco; the kids running me through all I had missed — glowing necklaces, Margot winning a shuffle dance war and Ella from year six snogging Harry (also from year six) in front of their mortified dads who, I hazarded a guess, had a worse evening than Henry.

Although from what I can gather, Henry didn't have such a bad time after all. It seems I wasn't the only wife who decided it was her husband's turn to step up and a small 'stitched-up dads' club formed in the corner of the hall next to the toilets, where they all stood slagging off the price of the glow sticks and taking it in turns to buy a round of coke at 80 pence a cup.

Just as we were heading to bed, Tara started acting a bit strange and so I opted to stay downstairs with her. An hour or so later, she took herself into her whelping box and what followed was a very long but straightforward labour which resulted in nine healthy pups.

Tara is a natural mum and very loving, nudging them as they wriggle and squeak. After weighing the pups today, I'm happy to be able to say that they've all gained weight and are looking perfect. The older children have seen them briefly but we have decided to not let the other children in to visit them for a few days until Tara is fully in the swing of things and relaxed.

A list of potential owners is waiting in the wings for them but they won't be able to visit until the puppies reach four weeks of age. It seems sad thinking about new owners for them already but we have a responsibility to make sure each pup has a caring, life-long home and that takes time.

Friday 20th February

11 a.m.

Hacked Burmese out this morning. He was quite well-behaved apart from being so strong. I felt we would possibly never stop as we cantered around the crop fields at the back of the house. He has also got into a twattish habit of spooking and pretending he is a poor frightened chap at everything he passes, which he most certainly is not. I need to spend some time in the next few weeks re-schooling him.

2 p.m.

Just got a parcel addressed to Margot Babylady. Being a respectful parent who values my children's privacy, I ripped it open immediately. I was more than a bit confused to be greeted with a cuddly toy and a letter congratulating Margot for pledging to adopt a snow leopard.

I walked back up to the house, dragging the wheelie bin

with me and admiring the gardens which had vastly improved since the weekly visits from the village gardener. The weeds were all but gone and the hedges that bordered the stables trimmed and shaped. According to Rose, one of the gardeners, by summer the farmhouse front will be an abundance of thick plum haze from the wisteria which, at the moment, although it blankets the whole farmhouse exterior, looks quite sorry for itself.

I kicked off my muck boots in the boot room and hung up my coat then walked into the kitchen, dumping Margot's box on the kitchen table before washing my hands and flicking on the coffee machine. As it sprang into life, Henry, who had been busy on the phone to one of his work contractors, joined me in the kitchen.

'You didn't mention you let Margot adopt a snow leopard?' I asked.

'I didn't. Why, who told you that?' he asked, looking puzzled.

I pushed the box towards him. 'Well, someone has, darling, and it isn't me. She received this today — a welcome letter and a cuddly toy. I wonder if she asked your dad to do it when they were here the other week?'

'No, it can't be my parents. Look, it's our direct debit details! Are you *sure* you didn't sign her up?' insisted Henry, waving the paperwork in my face.

'Of course I'm bloody sure. We'll just have to ask her when she comes home. I'm going to drink this coffee and go and collect them. I won't be long and the others are happy playing.'

'Yes, that's fine,' he said, looking over at Charles and Agatha who were playing with building blocks on the rug while Penny sat next to them, clapping her hands every time a tower toppled over. Henry pushed the box away, still shaking his head, then added, 'We need to find out how this has happened as soon as they get home and, more importantly, who used our card details. Good grief, I dread to think!'

5 p.m.

When the children came home they all dumped their bags in the hallway, flung off their school shoes, and headed to the kitchen, expecting the usual after-school hot chocolate and snacks to see them through until supper was ready. Instead they were all asked to sit around the table for a family meeting.

Henry opened the box and placed the contents on the table then asked calmly, 'Right, Mummy and I need to know if any of you have any idea how we've adopted a snow leopard using our bank card which, by the way, is against the law.'

Silence and a few side glances from Martha and Margot.

'You all know you are not allowed to order or buy anything online without permission. Now, we need to know who ordered this.'

Still silence.

'It wasn't me. If *I* was going to adopt an animal, I would choose a bear. I love bears,' shouted Edward.

'I would choose a goldfish. I love goldfish,' said Agatha.

Charles, who loves animals, then got very excited. 'I would have a goldfish and a guinea pig. I really want a guinea pig or a hamster. Can I have a guinea pig or a hamster as a pet?' he asked.

I was losing patience and so decided to help things along a bit. 'Charles, at the moment we need to talk about who ordered the snow leopard. Right, whoever tells me who ordered this, gets a cake!' I said, standing up and waving the leopard around.

'I know! I know! It was Margot and Martha, Mummy! They did it! I saw them when you were cutting up apples for our apple crumble. They used your laptop and it filled in all the numbers for them! Can I have a cake now?' shouted Etta, looking pleased with herself.

'She's lying! No, I didn't. Margot did it. I just watched her!' shouted Martha, before realising she had dropped herself and her sister in it while Margot sat, arms folded, staring at the fruit bowl.

'Why didn't you tell Mummy before?' I asked her.

'I did and you said, "That's nice, darling, pass Mummy the saucepan," so I did. Can I have a cake with icing on it, the cherry one?'

'Well, now we know the hows, whos and whys, we need to make a plan. I think it's fabulous that you both want to support endangered animals and so Mummy and I will make some weekly jobs for you both to complete in order to earn the £6 a month sponsor money, each and every month for the next year,' said Henry, half smiling, before turning to me and whispering,

'That's nice, darling, pass the saucepan,' while rolling his eyes and laughing.

'Okay, sorry, we just wanted to help the big cats before they all die out,' sniffed Margot.

Henry softened. 'Which is lovely of you but you must always ask Mum or me and not just do things like that on your own in future. And never use our cards without permission.'

'Mummy, can I have my cake now then for telling you who broke the bank law?' Etta asked again. That gave us all the giggles and I sent Nora into the pantry to get the cake tin. We then all, including the dogs, who are all partial to a slice of lemon sponge, sat together, chatting and eating every last piece of cake which, although delicious, almost certainly ruined our appetites for supper.

Saturday 21st February

Afternoon

We have another two new additions to the family, Porker and Sausage. Agatha named Porker because she was the biggest out of all the piglets and Henry named Sausage 'to remind us all why we have them.' They are Gloucestershire Old Spots and came from a local farm. We reserved them a few weeks ago but had to wait for all our paperwork to come through to show we have a license and that our farm is a registered smallholding.

Henry fenced a third of an acre of orchard for them, around

their pig ark that we got a few weeks back which the children layered with straw. There is a shallow mud bath for them to wallow in and lots of trees for natural shelter. You should see them — they're very intelligent and spend hours entertaining themselves with the footballs and horses treat toys we've put in the enclosure to keep them happy. I'm really fond of them already, as are the children, especially Charles who is utterly fascinated and sits with them for hours as they rummage around in the dirt for the fruit and vegetables he's buried for them to forage and find.

There's no way we shall ever be eating them; they have a home for life here. Henry has warmed to them as well. I actually caught him rubbing Porker's belly while saying, 'Ahh, you're a good little pig,' to her while he waited for their water troughs to fill up this morning. They're impossible not to warm to; as soon as they see you, they stop what they're doing and trot over, squeaking with excitement. They've also learned to play tag with Daisy and Nancy which is possibly the most entertaining thing I've ever seen.

Sunday 22nd February

1 p.m.

Just back from a hack with Agatha and Martha. I led Agatha on a lead rein from Burmese while Martha walked alongside Star and Nora. Margot crawled along behind us on a less than enthusiastic Roman. We had a little plod through the quiet lanes and then a slow trot around the crop fields before returning home via the village where the girls waved at several of their friends as we rode past their houses.

As cute as Tinker the Shetland pony is, he's a bit of a little shit to be honest with you. He has an aura about him that oozes 'I'm doing you all a massive favour' as he stomps along, ears back, letting out indignant sighs and taking his mood out on Roman by nipping her generous bottom every time the opportunity arises.

We've also discovered in the short time we've had Tinker that he's a bit of an escape artist and has broken out of his paddock countless times. Last week I actually found him in our kitchen, trying to eat out of the bin. Nora had tied him up and left him unattended while she looked for some hoof oil. Obviously bored of waiting, he untied himself and brazenly entered the house via the utility door then, when we found him, he planted himself to the spot and refused to move.

In the end he had to be dragged out by Martha tugging his lead rope and me giving him an encouraging tap on the bum with a broom handle. I've learned the hard way not to be close to his legs when he's having a strop. Despite all his faults, he's good with the children and far too fat and lazy to be spooky so, as far as a lead rein pony goes, he does his job, albeit through gritted teeth.

Star is a very different character and is a delight. The sweetest, kindest pony you could wish for. Apart from one mishap with a push bike, which caused her to dart forward and unseat Martha, she hasn't stepped a foot wrong. Since then, we've been working on making her more confident around bikes. The children ride past her the other side of the fence whilst she's in the paddock eating her dinner but, for now, Martha is walking alongside anyone who rides Star out with a lead rein, in case we come across anyone on a push bike, which is more likely than passing a tractor or car as it's so quiet here. Perfect riding country.

5 p.m.

The pool has finally had the heat pump fitted but we're waiting for our pool cover and alarm system which are being done this week. As expected, Henry wasn't impressed that we've been volunteered to host the school's swimming lessons in the summer term but we've agreed the school can use the pool on a Monday from ten until three with an hour break at lunch.

I've warmed to the idea as it would only be sitting there doing nothing anyway. Mr Plait sent out the swimming permission slips this week for classes to start after Easter (weather permitting) with a disclaimer basically saying the pool would be inspected each week, the deep end would be roped off and that Mrs Benson of class three has both first aid and life guard training and would be in sole charge of the lessons, along with two parent helpers, and that I am in no way responsible for any 'unfortunate events' should they occur. Which basically translates to if anyone drowns they cannot sue me. Fucking hell, please don't let anyone drown.

I think I'm going to volunteer to be an extra parent helper just to keep an eye on things. I've also agreed to provide a simple snack and drink in the changing room after swimming, which is a whole new dilemma. If it was just my kids, I would give them a Capri Sun, a token piece of fruit, and a packet of crisps or a Kit Kat, but I doubt that's allowed now after Jamie Oliver and his school meal campaigns. I'll have to ask Florence; she's provided enough government-approved snacks as part of the PTA over the years. She's bound to know these things.

Tuesday 24th February

Phone call from Suzie, the leader of Agatha and Charles's pre-school. 'Hello, Alice, it's Suzie here. Nothing to worry about, your little angels are fine. I just wanted to have a little chat with you, if you have a moment?' My heart sank at this point. No one would ever describe Agatha and Charles as angels because, as cute as they are, they also have a tendency to be mischievous. So either Suzie wanted something or Agatha had told her the story of Edward climbing onto the stable roof at the weekend.

Fuck's sake, I thought before responding. 'Hi, Suzie, yes I have a moment. What did you want to talk about?' I asked, dreading the answer.

'Well, I have a favour to ask. Now don't feel you have to

say yes but I've been speaking to some of the teachers over at the main school and they've mentioned you've kindly agreed to let them use your swimming pool when the weather warms up. So please don't feel I'm putting you on the spot but I was speaking to my helpers here about it and, well, we wondered if you could extend your kindness to us at the pre-school? It would be such an amazing treat for the children and, well, they would be learning a vital life skill,' said Suzie.

'Yes, of course, you're most welcome to use it. Mr Plait has arranged to come on a Monday from ten until three but any other day would be fine,' I replied.

'Well, we have a full house here on a Thursday afternoon so, if we could pencil in from twelve until two in the afternoon, that would be great. Only if that suits you?'

I found myself agreeing and adding I would also supply some snacks and drinks as I'll be doing so to the school children. I can't moan really though as Agatha has been a bit difficult lately at pre-school, mainly due to her new obsession with the colour red. It started with a red pair of Ladybird shoes I picked up for her in Next which she took a major liking to. This then extended to wanting matching red socks and then red clothing. She is now completely obsessed.

Red aprons, red lunch box, red pens, everything she has, has to be red, which is causing some issues both at pre-school and home, usually in the form of a meltdown which has now become known as a code red. Things came to a head the other day, causing Suzie to make Agatha a red (obviously) badge saying 'I ONLY WEAR RED APRONS' after a new member of staff, unaware of Agatha's strong colour preferences, gave her a blue apron. Cue a 'code red' situation from my outraged, curly-haired toddler.

From what I can gather from the report that Suzie, who is lucky enough to be her key leader as well as the pre-school manager, gave me, Agatha, having been offered an apron of the non-red variety, refused point blank to wear it so the new helper told her she couldn't play in the make and create corner if she didn't put it on.

This sent Agatha, who is partial to a good make and create session, over the edge. The staff then looked on dumbfounded while Agatha, aka Emily Rose, proceeded to scream, 'I DON'T WEAR BLUE APRONS,' and stomped off to the home corner where she started to headbutt the toy kitchen while launching various pieces of plastic food and plates at anyone who dared venture within throwing distance of her. When there was nothing left to throw, she sat stamping her feet on the wall while screeching, 'I ONLY WEAR RED,' until a red apron was found. She then stood up, put it on, and indignantly declared, 'That's all I wanted! I'm going to play with my brother now!' and waltzed over to the water table, sidled up to Charles, where she then stood playing with boats like nothing had happened.

In short, she's an absolute nightmare at the moment and so their request for a few free hours use of our swimming pool once a week is not really something I could turn down.

Thursday 25th February

11 a.m.

The puppies are thriving. I can't believe how much they've changed in such a short space of time. I'm going to email all the responses I've got from our advert on Champdogs. I'm shocked by the amount of potential new owners who have contacted us already. I'm sure they won't all be suitable though so now it's time to start sifting through them.

Evening

Just had a bit of a row with Henry after he wrongly accused me of being too fussy over potential new puppy owners. He's come to this untrue conclusion after he read an email I wanted to send to all of them. He believes me asking them if any of their family members will be looking after the pups at any time in the future and, if so, could I have their contact details, is a bit OTT specially as I go on to request photographs of their gardens and a character reference from a vet or character report from another professional if they happen to be first-time owners, which he believes is 'borderline obsessive and mental'.

Friday 26th February

Morning

Came to an agreement with my insulting husband. We've emailed all the potential owners together. I wasn't overly happy that Henry wouldn't let me ask as many questions as I would like but I guess it's better to meet people in the flesh and see how the dogs take to them, so I sent a 'less off-putting' email:

Dear xxx,

Thank you for expressing your interest in our litter of puppies. They are ready to leave the weekend of the 13th of April. They will come with all of their pedigree paper work; a vet wellness check together with a worming, microchip and vaccination card and a puppy pack.

These puppies are very special to us and are being raised with love in our family countryside home with other animals and children who adore them.

Therefore we will only be agreeing homes for these puppies when we have met potential owners in person on a visit at a mutually agreeable time to ensure the puppies are right for you and vice versa.

We are able to take visits after the 14th March. If you would like to visit, please reply when you would like to do so, telling us a little bit about yourself and your family, if you have owned dogs previously and whether you are looking for a male or female.

Best wishes,

Alice and Henry Babylady

Evening

We have six people arranged to visit the pups. They're a real mix — families with children, an older couple, a farmer looking for a companion around his farm, to name a few. They all seem like nice people. On paper anyway. We're going to start making a heated puppy play den in one of the stables so we can move them out there in the daytime when they reach three weeks old and commence weaning them. Then, when they reach four weeks, they'll move out there full-time with Tara and come into the house in small groups throughout the day for cuddles and socialising.

MARCH

Monday 1st March

Henry has just got back from a weekend away with work so I've been on my own with all eight children (one of which kept me up all night teething and then clinging to me all day, making my thousand and one jobs even harder), Burmese (who always likes to choose his moments went lame yesterday and had to be seen by the farrier, who thankfully sorted him out), three ponies (one of which keeps fucking escaping like Houdini), The MIL (who spent all of yesterday incensed that Waitrose sent Princes tuna in sunflower oil as an alternative to her usual Waitrose tuna steak in spring water), four dogs, nine puppies (who are as demanding as eight toddlers), the best of the lot were Sausage and Porker.

So I wasn't in the best of moods when Henry walked in (looking suspiciously tanned for someone who had been in Dubai 'strictly for business'), took one look around the kitchen/day room and asked, 'Wooow, what's been going on here? What a shithole! Have you been on strike, darling, or have we been raided?'

I was keen to bring him up to speed on exactly what I've been doing and how, no, we hadn't 'been raided' nor had I been 'on strike'; in fact I hadn't stopped for three days and nights but what an excellent idea a strike was. I then abandoned ship, leaving him to occupy the children and cook supper while I locked myself in our bathroom.

Despite our grand plans for a new bathroom suite, it hasn't yet changed at all; it's still very much Scar Face central. Quinn said last time he was in there he feels that piles of cocaine on the sides would be more suited than the basket of bath toys and many bottles of baby shampoo but added, 'It's very Versace.' It's not my taste but the sunken bath is just like the one in *Pretty Woman*, albeit in black marble and faux gold taps, and so, while not as stylish as my old bathroom, the deep bath is bliss and, once you light a few candles, add some bath oil and sink in with a good book, it's pretty much heaven.

Thursday 4th March

I've made some really good friends at book club. We only seem to briefly stay on the subject of books as we all have so many other things in common. The conversation always seems to drift away from our current read and on to our own lives. I always have a really good time. A few of the ladies are also part of the PTA which makes the (what seem like) constant meetings much more fun.

We have a meeting tonight, in fact, which should have been on Tuesday but Mr Plait moved it so Quinn, who has been in the Maldives, didn't miss out. Another random development is that Amanda is now trying to befriend me though I'm struggling to have much time for her given how she was with me in the weeks after I first met her. I've decided to try to be friends with her as it's nicer for everyone, including us, if we can get on. She's shown an interest in Burmese after seeing me hack him around the village; turns out she's a very accomplished horsewoman herself and is keen to ride him.

Normally I wouldn't even consider it but she used to ride racehorses in training and assures me she will cope with him. We are going to arrange for her to come and have a try on him before I let her loose in open country or disembark her onto the village.

Saturday 6th March

Evening

Friday evening and today has been super. Henry and I don't hide the fact we are obsessive dog lovers which has, in turn, rubbed off on the little people and so the fact it's Crufts season has given the farmhouse an upbeat buzz.

In true English fashion, the weather has been drizzling

non-stop all week so we spent Friday evening watching the show's highlights while eating oven-roasted chicken in crusty rolls then warm, winter-fruit crumble with vanilla custard that I picked up from a local farm shop, while lounging around our day room (which has become our all-the-time room), placing bets on who we believed would win each category. Astonishingly Edward was choosing the winner of every single category so, in my usual competitive nature, I decided to try to get some pointers. While dishing him a second helping of crumble, I pulled him to one side and asked him what made him choose the dogs he had and how he decided they would win to which he shrugged his shoulders, gave the vague response of, 'It's just that extra-special aura they give off, Mum. If you see it, you see it; if you don't, you don't.'

I now feel like my six-year-old has a more complex mind than me.

Sunday 7th March

Spent all day preparing for our very own Crufts Best in Show tomorrow. Martha, Charles, and Etta have been making rosettes using a mixture of my art paper (which I've had for the last four years and, up until this morning, was still packaged, patiently waiting for when I had time to start painting again), a selection of glitter glue and so-called washable pens (which I can sadly say are not at all washable and I have two pen-striped Orla Kiely bed sets to prove it), and some ribbon which I had previously used to plait Etta and Agatha's hair in old-fashioned, plaited bunches.

Meanwhile Edward and Henry set to, making our meadow field into a dog agility course using a selection of horse jumps, hay bales, wheelie bins, a garden slide and anything else they found lying around. I am, and always will be, the organiser of the family so myself and Nora (my second in command) wrote the rules out and the team information:

Competitors' Information

Teams have been drawn at random (wasn't at all at random but it saved the arguments as to who wanted to be on whose team) are as follows:

Team one - Edward, Charles and Martha.

Team two - Etta, Margot, Nora and Agatha.

Each team will work together to complete one round of agility with their chosen dog.

Each team will take a short break and enjoy a buffet lunch and refreshments. They will then take part in Best in Show.

Each team will then appoint two teammates to compete in Best in Show and will have the choice of three dogs to show. They will be scored out of five, based on the team's control, showing style, and how well-groomed the dog is.

Good Luck. And remember, choose your dog wisely and, most importantly, NO MOANING, TANTRUMS,

KICKING, OR HITTING EACH OTHER AND WHAT THE JUDGE SAYS IS FINAL!!!

This left Margot and Agatha (a very worrying combination at the best of times) to write a list of prizes. Having decided to give prizes that we could give for free, they actually, to my surprise, came up with some good ones:

PRIZES FOR THE BABYLADY DOG SHOW OF THE YEAR

First prize for agility competition — Breakfast in bed for the winners, cooked and served by the losers.

First prize for Best in Show — The winners for Best in Show must be treated like kings or queens for a whole morning and be waited on hand and foot by the losers! And anything that isn't dangerous must be carried out without moaning!

With the teams and rules set, we all gathered outside. Penny happily sat in her buggy, eating raisins, while Burmese and the ponies stopped grazing and plodded over to the gate and looked on with interest, no doubt sensing something out of the ordinary was about to occur. The weather, for the first time this week, was on our side and although the ground was still wet from the last few days' rain, the sun decided to make an appearance.

'Right, everyone, get in your teams and we will flip a coin to see who goes first,' shouted Henry.

For once the children did as they were told and listened carefully to the game instructions. The coin flip meant Martha, Edward and Charles, who had named their team 'Doberman', were up first. They interestingly announced they had opted to have Nancy as their team dog. When I say it was an interesting decision, I mean mental decision because, as kind and tolerant of the children as Nancy is and the fact she follows the children round like a lost sheep all day and sleeps by their beds, she is also a very naughty and disobedient dog.

Nancy is also now weighing in at over 60 kilos so it could be argued she's far from built for agility and, given her stubborn personality, she won't be persuaded to do anything she doesn't want to do.

'Are you sure you want to have Nancy?' I asked, pulling a confused face.

'Yes, Mum, we are sure!' they all bellowed back.

Martha went to retrieve Nancy who followed behind her excitedly. I could barely believe my eyes as Nancy trotted like a show pony and heaved her massive bulk over the jumps and weaved in and out of the wheelie bins, following Edward who had taken the role of pathfinder. It was mesmerizing. Henry and I gave each other bemused looks, not quite believing what we had just seen. They finished their course with no refusals in 4 minutes 21 seconds.

'Right, well done, Team Doberman! Now it's the turn of

Team Two (who had called themselves Bichon Frise). Which dog will your team be completing the course with?' I asked.

'Bichon Frise will be having Daisy!' shouted Margot.

Now this will be interesting, I thought.

Team Bichon Frise didn't have the same good luck as Team Doberman. In fact they never got past the first jump after Daisy decided she would rather lie on her back and have her belly rubbed then darted off to chase a rabbit she spotted by the pond. After many failed attempts to retrieve her, Team Bichon Frise received a penalty and swapped to Chubb who, although stubborn and furious to be away from his beloved sofa, completed the course in 5 minutes 11 seconds, led by Nora and encouraged by Margot and Agatha. Etta opted to shout instructions from the side lines.

We all then retreated back to the farmhouse for a break and tucked into steak sandwiches and cheesy chips then sipped on banana milkshakes; not the healthiest of meals but we all live an active enough life not to worry about the odd treat day.

Henry and I then gave the children half an hour to brush their chosen dog and practice their Best in Show performance while he loaded the dishwasher and I bathed Penny who, having enjoyed her lunch, was head to toe in ketchup and had pieces of melted cheese in her hair.

Then after I put Penny to bed for a nap, switching on the baby monitor as I crept out and joined Henry at the makeshift show ring which had been created with hay bales in a square. The children were all sitting on them in their teams, awaiting their big moment.

Team Bichon Frise had appointed Agatha and Etta as chief handlers for the Best in Show.

'Please could you introduce your dog, Team Bichon Frise, and tell your audience a bit more about her?' Henry said, smiling at a beaming Agatha and Etta who were now standing in the centre, proudly holding the lead of a less-than-thrilled Chubb.

'This is Chubb. He is a Chow Chow and he has a blue tongue. He loves Tic Tacs and being lazy and he snores an awful lot. He has been groomed today by my sister, Nora,' said Etta.

'Nora, please could you tell the audience what grooming techniques you have applied to Chubb to prepare him for today's show?' Henry asked.

Nora shyly stood up and joined her sisters in the ring. 'Today I've brushed Chubb using a dog brush mitt and sprayed him with dog dry shampoo.'

'And an excellent job you have done!' I said, smiling at Nora. 'Now who is going to be handling your dog today?'

'Agatha and Etta are our chosen handlers, under the supervision of Nora and I,' replied Margot, who was taking the competition very seriously.

'Right, okay then. I will inspect your dog so please hold him still,' I laughed.

I then walked over to Chubb as Etta held his lead in one hand and Agatha's hand in her other. I noticed Agatha's other hand was behind her back and her fingers were crossed for luck.

I ran my hands down Chubb's back and then inspected his eyes and teeth and then said brightly, 'Excellent work, girls. Now please could you trot him up and down so I can see how he moves?'

Etta and Agatha wasted no time in carefully running alongside, kindly patting Chubb and telling him what a good boy he was. Chubb, who has always been partial to a bit of ego boosting, decided he actually loved being a show dog after all and wagged his tail as he jumped around excitedly.

'Brilliant performance from the Bichon Frise Team now could Team Doberman join us ringside?' shouted Henry, bringing the clapping to a close.

Team Doberman darted into the centre of the ring with an over-excited Nancy who seemed rather too eager for her usual Eeyore-like self.

'Please could you tell us all who will be handling your dog today?' I asked, still trying to work out why Nancy was so interested in Edward.

'I will be Nancy's handler today!' said Edward, cockily smirking,

'Could you tell me a bit more about your dog, Martha?' Henry asked.

'Well, she's called Nancy. She's a Mastiff and is loving every moment of show life!' said a very confident Martha.

'Charles, who groomed Nancy today?' I asked, still watching Nancy obsessively hover around Edward.

'No one; we tried to wipe her with wet wipes but she kept

trying to eat them!' he replied, laughing.

'Ah, that's it. Thank you, Charles,' Henry muttered to himself.

I repeated the same judge inspection to Nancy who still seemed more interested in Edward than me or anyone else around her.

'Right, please trot up your dog!' I said, still laughing at how weirdly Nancy was behaving. Nancy stayed so close to Edward as he trotted her up, she reminded me of a highly trained sheepdog.

Everyone clapped them as they joined Team Bichon Frise on the bales. I noticed Henry speaking to Margot and Nora quietly and a big grin appeared across their faces.

He joined me in the centre of the ring as Etta passed the baskets of rosettes to me.

'Well, what a fun day it's been. We've seen some excellent performances from both teams and you've both done extremely well, so congratulations to all of you. Who's had a good time?'

Everyone chanted, 'ME!' as they raised their hands.

'Time for the awards. The winners of the agility, as you know, were Team Doberman!'

Everyone clapped; even the losers took it in good spirit.

Henry continued, 'Now for the Best in Show. Team Doberman scored four points as they lost one point for having an ungroomed dog. Bichon Frise are the clear winners as they've scored top marks, with perfect and kind handling from Etta and Agatha, alongside coaching from Margot and immaculate grooming, thanks to Nora.'

Etta and Agatha looked proud as punch and hugged each other while Margot and Nora gave each other high fives. Henry continued, 'It would have been one win for each side. However, first, Margot has a stewards enquiry to raise.'

Margot stood up. 'On behalf of my team, I wish to report Doberman Team for cheating! We believe they have cheated in both competitions and so they should be disqualified,' she said, not quite hiding her glee.

'Please could you provide any evidence or reasons for accusing Team Doberman of cheating?' I asked, trying not to laugh as it all fell into place in my own mind.

'Yes, we can,' said Nora. 'Edward has food in his pockets! That's why Nancy is behaving. She's following Edward for treats!'

'Is this true, Team Doberman?' Henry asked before adding, 'In fact, perhaps you could join me in the ring and empty your pockets?'

As they stepped into the ring, Martha was no longer smug, perhaps realising she had a busy morning cooking breakfast and waiting on her sisters to come. As expected, Edward had eight slices of ham and two pieces of cooked, crispy bacon (left over from breakfast) in his trouser pockets, which Nancy dived to hoover up as it fell to the floor.

'Team Doberman, as ingenious as your cheating was, you are disqualified and therefore Edward, Charles and Martha will be making Team Bichon Frise breakfast in bed and will spend the rest of the morning treating the winning team like queens and catering to their every wish!' laughed Henry.

'Losers! I'm going to make you massage my feet while spoon feeding me ice cream!' gloated a delighted Margot.

'Etta and me want bacon and pancakes for breakfast, on a tray with a flower in a glass and a pink napkin,' joined in Agatha.

'And you can clean all our bedrooms!' chirped up Nora. 'This is going to be brilliant!'

From the looks on team Doberman's faces, they didn't share Nora's enthusiasm.

Wednesday 9th March

Martha took invites for the whole school to come to an Easter hunt at the farmhouse next month, not for any reason other than we just fancied a party now the better weather is here.

The school is so small and, with us having children in so many year groups, it would be cruel to only invite some of the children in each class, leaving some left out. I remember how my girls have felt being left out of party invites over the years and the tears they've shed over it so we've thrown caution to the wind and invited all 70-odd pupils and extended the invite to siblings.

The thought of so many children running riot has brought Henry out in a cold sweat but he came around when I suggested making the house out of bounds due to the dogs and puppies, and proposed having gazebos and using the toilet in the swimming pool changing rooms. He's now helping with the arrangements.

We're going to have a bouncy castle. Jean is coming with two of her grooms who have the correct qualifications and insurance so are going to give pony rides on Tinker, Roman and Star. Henry has a friend that supplies boxes of Easter eggs at trade price so we've placed a large order and I've booked a company to come in to serve a hog roast and set up a bar for the adults, and milkshakes, cordials and ice creams for the children. We are all really looking forward to it.

Sunday 12th March

7:30 a.m.

Penny is still teething and then so Henry and I have just had words over his selective hearing last night (and every fucking night). There is no way he doesn't hear Penny crying; he simply chooses to ignore her while waiting for me to go to her, which I always do, every single time.

Well, last night, after the hundredth time out of bed, I reached my limit so decided to wait it out, which turned into a silent stand-off. I knew Henry could hear Penny and he knew I knew he could hear her but he still just lay there! Not being a self-centred fuck like Henry and because I couldn't stand it anymore, I got up in a huge huff and stropped out to get her, not before turning on the en suite light and giving the end of the bed a kick.

I woke up this morning still seething and so Henry gave me the perfect opportunity to snap when he sat up and yawned and actually had the audacity to stretch and say, 'Cor, I'm so tired. I had a terrible night.'

This made me see red. 'Pardon? You had what?' I demanded, glaring at him.

'Oh, I know you're tired as well. I was just saying I'm really tired still this morning,' he stammered, backpedalling.

'As well? As well as what? As well as me, the one who got up with Penny all night while you pretended not to hear her because you're a selfish bloody bastard?' I demanded, feeling my blood boil. Nothing like a good dose of sleep deprivation to send me more than slightly mental.

'I didn't hear her, darling,' he said sheepishly.

'Don't you "darling" me! You did, you liar. Well, if you think I'm cooking breakfast for everyone while you sit and read the bastard papers, yawning into your coffee cup and acting hard done by after nine hours' solid sleep, you can piss off!' I raged.

I'm now sulking in bed, listening to him try and fail to get the children organised for breakfast. He sounds really stressed which makes me feel a bit better. I'll give it another five minutes then go and help.

Evening

This weekend has been manic. We had paving contractors here laying non-slip tiles around the swimming pool which meant, although the dogs and children couldn't get in there and walk on their hard work because it's enclosed, they could however stand at the picket fence and shout endless questions and have a chat with them (children) and sit guarding and barking every time the workers came anywhere near the kids (Daisy and Nancy).

I think the workmen may possibly now be in need of at least a week off to lie in a quiet dark room after the hours upon hours they've endured, listening to Agatha's and Etta's in-depth, graphic and mostly inappropriate stories while Charles reeled off everything he knows about guinea pigs, over and over again (which is enough to make me, his own doting mother, glaze over let alone poor Jim and Don from Garden Magic Ltd). Bless them, they were very friendly, nodding at the kids and politely declining Margot's offer to help cut the paving with their angle grinder while they drank their cups of coffee.

They've done a grand job though, despite the audience and the pool is now all ready to be used. The cover is on and the water's heating up as I type. The children are fit to burst with excitement in anticipation of having their first swim.

The puppy play den is another big achievement this weekend and is now all ready for its new residents. Henry has steam-cleaned the end stable which was used as a storeroom and had a kennel heater fitted by the village electrician. It already has a window for ventilation and has a stable door (obviously) so will have plenty of air flow in the daytime. We've also set up Harrison fencing to enclose the stable door and a good-sized piece of land to create a secure outdoor area on both hardstanding and grass, which will be nice for the puppies as they get older.

For now we have a varnished MDF board that can be secured during the day inside the stable door entrance to keep the pups in but low enough for Tara to be able to hop over to have some time away from them if she wants to or to go to the toilet. At night we can remove it and close the door. Inside looks brilliant. Paper-based, dust-free, shredded bedding has been laid on top of rubber matting for their comfort and to absorb the inevitable mess nine puppies make. It's ideal floor covering as we can easily change it a few times a day.

We have two XXXL plastic dog beds lined with Vetbed which will provide more than enough room for mum and all her babies. They have a play area with children's play tunnels, a plastic toddler outdoor toy that has circles cut out of it for them to crawl through, baby-safe teddy bears, lightweight footballs, chew toys and what will become the most important thing in their lives in the coming weeks — a weaning feed trough along the back wall with twelve head spaces, which is more than enough room for them all to get food without having to compete for it.

Henry has also screwed to the wall at their head height four water trays so they'll always have a constant source of fresh water. We're going to move mum and babies up there tomorrow and see how they get on. I've just popped my head in there after putting Roman and Burmese to bed and it's pleasantly warm thanks to the heater and the low watt safety light that was also fitted makes it really cosy.

Monday 13th March

First day for Tara and the puppies up at the stables and they seem to love the new setup. Tara has spent most of the day sleeping in one of the beds while the puppies follow the constantly re-occurring cycle of rough playing with each other and the toys, drinking from the ever-open, mummy milk bar (milk drunk in all manner of positions), then falling asleep, before waking up and starting the cycle again.

Wednesday 15th March

6 p.m.

Florence just phoned with some bad — actually, fucking terrible — news.

'Darling, I wish I could say I've phoned for a catch-up but I'm here with Sarah and Fiona and we've some pretty disgusting news. That bastard Mario, that dirty bloody bastard, has been at it again!' exclaimed Florence.

'Oh no, does Beth know?' I sighed sadly.

'No, darling, she doesn't. We wanted to discuss it with you first.'

'Are you sure about Mario?' I asked.

'Sadly, yes. Fiona's sister saw him coming out of the Rochester Hotel snogging the tart's face off yesterday morning and, knowing what a shit he is, she had the sense to take a photo of them and sent it to Fiona so he couldn't worm his way out of it.'

'That bloody shit! I can't believe he's done it again,' I said, fuming.

'What to do, do you think, darling?' Florence asked.

'Well, we can't keep it from Beth. She needs to know. You'll have to go and show her the evidence.'

8 p.m.

Henry and I aren't speaking. When I told him about Mario cheating, he didn't seem surprised so I asked him if he knew about it and he replied, 'Well, I had an inkling, yes, but I didn't want to get involved,' which means he knew and kept it from me. Fuming!

9 p.m.

Florence has been around to Beth and told her. Beth's upset but wants to speak to Mario and see what he has to say. I have a horrible feeling she will let him get away with it again, which is why he continues to do it. Regardless of her decision, I'll support her because that's what friends do but if Henry cheated on me, that would be it. What's a relationship built on if you can't trust each other? Poor Beth, what a horrible position to be in.

Henry and I are talking again. I can see why he wanted to stay out of it but I'm still a bit annoyed he didn't tell me; after all, Beth is his friend more than Mario is. Henry only sodding well knows him because he's Beth shithead husband.

We very nearly fell out again when I said, 'Mario can get fucked now (perhaps not the best choice of wording, given the situation). We are Team Beth all the way.'

'Well, darling, it's not really our place to take sides, is it? We can be friends with both of them, whatever happens, can't we?'

I lost my cool a bit again at his idiotic remark and scrunched up my nose and pulled a face that said 'are you fucking stupid?' before replying, 'Of course we can't be friends with them both! You have to pick a side! I obviously will back Beth which means, as my husband, so do you.' I do wonder sometimes... We left it at that.

Friday 17th March

Just got an email which was also copied in to Florence, Fiona and Sarah:

Hi Girls,

Thank you for being honest with me and letting me know what you found out about Mario. I know you would have found it difficult.

Mario and I have spoken at length and he's admitted it all and said he knows he is wrong and so we're going to give things another go. I know you'll think I'm stupid but I really love him and, in all honesty, would be lost without him so I've resigned myself that this is just how it is and accepted that I'll just have to put up with his indiscretions. I will have to learn to live with it.

You all know as well as I do there have been many before his latest one and I would be lying to myself not to admit I know there will be many more but I've made the decision to stay with him, regardless of what he does because, well, I can't imagine life without him.

So if you hear any more about what he's been up to in the future, please don't tell me. I would rather not know.

Love you all,

Beth.

Possibly the saddest thing I have ever read. She deserves so much more.

Sunday the 18th March

Lots of visitors at the farm this weekend to visit us and the pups. Puppies are much like newborns, they seem to change and develop almost daily. It's amazing to see.

The first couple had two children around Martha and Etta's age and had travelled four hours to visit us. In their mid-40s, they were very chatty while their girls played with ours. They've reserved our biggest, most confident girl as their new family pet to join their friendly Labrador.

Shortly after waving them off, Dr Jenson arrived with his very pretty wife, Beatrice. Tara warmed to them instantly, nudging them both for fuss gently with her nose which is always a good sign.

We sat talking for well over an hour. They then left happily after reserving a laidback boy who our children have nicknamed Wiggle Bum. After lunch a retired gentleman arrived with his partner. They both wasted no time in getting to know the puppies. They sat on the floor and were flooded by excited pups. Despite being spoilt for choice, they had soon chosen their pup — a male who had really taken a shine to them both.

The last visit of the day wasn't so successful. Henry and I had assumed the people had decided not to come then, nearly two hours later than scheduled, they arrived, buzzing the gates impatiently just as we were about to sit down to supper. Having children ourselves, we gave them the benefit of the doubt, knowing they might have been held up en route. Henry volunteered to deal with them while I carried on feeding the children and starting bath and story time.

I might've agreed but was a bit miffed to be honest and felt a bit put out these people turned up so late. I had just cleared the dinner plates and was running the children's baths when I heard the kitchen patio door shut and, shortly after, footsteps coming up the stairs.

'Darling, they've gone,' said Henry flatly.

'That was quick. I thought you would be ages.'

'Yes, it didn't go well. I told them they wouldn't be having one of the pups. They didn't even address the fact they were hours late then the chap went to light a rollup right next to the stables, right adjacent to the hay bales, which put me off a bit, but the final nail in the coffin was their feral children trying to roughly pick up the puppies by their necks while they both stood by oblivious, asking me for a discount if they 'paid cash and didn't bother with the injections and all the other stupid crap'. Needless to say, that was enough for me and I asked them to leave.'

'What did you say to them?' I asked, shocked.

'I told them straight. Remove your children away from my dogs immediately and under no circumstances would we consider homing a pup with them when their main concern was having a cheap deal and not the welfare of the animal. And I added they should perhaps look into educating themselves and their children before even thinking about attempting to purchase another pup, or any other animal for that matter. I then said I'd buzz them out and have a safe journey.'

'Well, you've done right, darling. Well done.' I was pleased Henry hadn't beaten around the bush.

'Thank you. If you can manage here, I'll go and eat my cottage pie now. Is it in the Aga?'

I could hardly refuse really, could I? Not after him fending off those horrible people, so I ended up bathing all the kids and doing story time while Henry ate his cottage pie in front of the TV in peace. Some maybe would say it was a hero's reward.

The following day we had another whole day of puppy visits and I'm happy to say all the pups are now reserved to really good people. Each one of them has a very different life ahead of them but I'm confident they will all be equally happy and cared for.

Tuesday 20th March

10 a.m.

Nearly the whole school has already RSVP'd to the party; out of 61 replies, only 3 can't make it. Haven't told Henry yet. I will give him a few more days believing that probably at least half of the children we invited won't be able to come. Ignorance is bliss and all that.

I'm looking forward to the children getting home as the pool water has been tested this morning and the chemical levels are finally safe and the temperature is perfect. Henry told them it still wasn't ready this morning so it will be a nice surprise for them this afternoon. He's currently inflating some pool toys including a three-person floating, bright pink flamingo that will no doubt be the cause of some major arguments between the girls.

7:30 p.m.

Apart from Martha, the kids are all asleep. The pool was a huge hit, even if there were a few heated rows leading to Nora having to be dragged off Margot after Nora took exception to her jumping in before dipping her feet in the foot-cleansing bath. As expected the flamingo had to be removed after Henry finally had enough of repeatedly saying, 'Share it or it comes out of the pool! I will not tell you all again!'

It was well worth listening to the bickering given how tired they all were afterwards. It was brilliant. They came in, wrapped in dressing gowns; the girls had their hair wrapped in towels and they all ate their suppers without the usual 'I don't like this!' or 'I wanted chips'. Charles even fell asleep eating his pasta bake. Everyone went straight up to have a bath and hair wash then climbed into their PJs and into bed without a single objection. Agatha and Etta had fallen asleep before I'd even read page four of *The Suitcase Kid*, their current favourite book. Charles was so exhausted he didn't even want to have a rundown of guinea pig facts, which is a first, and Penny fell asleep on Martha's bed, watching *Peppa Pig* on Margot's laptop.

Henry is just outside, checking the animals and giving the

puppies the last feed of the day. I'm going to wait for the load of towels and dressing gowns I've just put in the washing machine to finish so I can hang them to dry before going to bed myself to read, while Henry watches some action film he's dying to see on the bedroom TV.

I was speaking to Henry earlier about how well the children have adapted to our new life; they really seem to love it and we certainly do. When we first moved here, I had a list of things I wanted to change to make the farmhouse more perfect and, dare I say, flashy, but I haven't changed a single thing. It's perfect just how it is.

It may not be as flashy as our old home and it does have taps that leak, a kitchen that's seen better days, chipped skirting boards and a mismatch of furniture but we are all so much more relaxed living in this house. It suits us much better. I didn't even end up painting Henry's office after he declared it 'perfect for him as is' which sums up Puddle-Duck Farm; not perfect but perfect for us.

Thursday 22nd March

Evening

Last night a miracle happened. Penny slept through again! I can now say it's not a fluke. Ever since the kids have been swimming after school, bedtime has been so much easier. Life is good. The last three nights are the first full night's sleep I've had in almost two years. I feel like a new woman.

Friday 23rd March

Amanda came to ride Burmese after school today. You may remember she had told me all about her experience with racehorses and her childhood ponies. Well, where do I even start?

She certainly looked the part in cream breeches, glossy leather show boots, and white competition blouse with a gold horseshoe clip through the buttonhole. I did think a hairnet and carrying a velvet hunting jacket was perhaps, as Henry would say, a bit 'too extra' for a hack around the village, but each to their own. I'd decided to let her take Roman who has two speeds — start and stop — while I would ride Burmese. Amanda was a bit disappointed, saying she wasn't too keen on 'carthorses' and was used to hot bloods with 'a bit of spirit'.

I knew something was up when I had tacked up Burmese and put on his exercise boots and Amanda had yet to enter Roman's stable. Roman does have a tendency to be a bit 'mareish' in the stable; nothing too terrible, just a bit of face pulling and will swing her bum around to guard her haynet. But put it this way, Martha can happily feed her and tack her up in the stable.

'Is everything okay, Amanda?' I asked, looking at Roman's bridle and saddle which were still in the same place I'd left them ten minutes earlier.

'Not really, no, she doesn't like me,' said Amanda quietly.

'Oh, don't take it personally. She's a bit grumpy which, given her age, we can forgive her for. Do you want me to tack her up for you?' I asked.

'How old is she? And, yes, I think that would be better if you did it,' Amanda said.

'She's almost 30, not that you would believe it, and she's a very kind mare; she really looks after her riders'. I replied as I stood next to Roman and popped the reins over her head then gently guided her bit in her almost toothless mouth. 'Thankfully she still manages to eat hay and loves her sugarbeet and Keyflow mashes so she's always been easy to keep the weight on,' I said as I tightened Roman's girth and led her out of her stable. 'Here you go. The mounting block is just by the gate. You may want to check the girth before you hop on,' I said as I handed Amanda the reins.

I could tell by the way she stared back at me blankly she had no idea what I was talking about. Just as I was contemplating what to do, Martha, Agatha and Margot appeared.

'Hi, Mum. Dad said we have to see what jobs we need to do before we go swimming!' said Agatha in her usual upbeat, happy way.

'Oh hello, girls. Well I've actually done most of the jobs but if you and Margot would like to play with the puppies while I'm gone and make sure they have fresh water, that would be a great help,' I said, smiling at Agatha.

'Okay then,' they both chorused.

'What about me, Mum?' asked Martha.

'Well, actually, I do have a job for you. Could you put your hat on and grab a lead rein? Amanda hasn't ridden for a while and so it may be a good idea for you to walk alongside Roman and help Amanda with her girth and things?'

'Yes, I will but I thought Amanda could ri— Oh, okay then, yes I'll get my hat,' responded Martha after seeing my look that said 'please do not question me'.

Ten minutes or so later, Amanda had heaved herself onto Roman and, after Martha had 'reminded' her how to hold the reins, we set off. Burmese was in his usual naughty mood and danced around on the spot impatiently, which didn't help poor Amanda's nerves which, judging by her pale face and lack of conversation, weren't holding up too well as it was.

Then a tractor turned into the lane towards us and, in true Burmese fashion, he began to heat up, jogging on the spot. I've found, after owning him for many years, the best course of action is no action at all, other than to maintain bit contact to keep his mind engaged and giving him the odd reassuring pat. As soon as Amanda spotted the tractor, she let out an ear-piercing scream and bellowed, 'ARGH, I AM GOING TO DIEEEE!' as the tractor approached us. Thankfully Roman is one of the very few horses around, where the dangerously overused phrase 'boobproof' really does apply. She is a pony in a million and stood still like a rock, even with a woman on her back screeching like a demented banshee.

After that episode Martha attached the lead rope and walked next to Amanda like she does with her little brothers and sisters. We made it back in one peace. I texted Amanda just now and suggested next week we swim instead, to which she replied:

I think that may be a better idea. I seem to have lost my nerve since having the boys and Katie. I don't think riding is for me anymore. I'm a bit rusty! xx

A bit rusty? I thought. *That's one word for it!* I have to say, I've warmed to Amanda after this afternoon. I find her really funny and ballsy and she took it on the chin despite how embarrassing it must have been to be led on a scruffy cob by a ten-year old, through the village, passing the residents, many of whom were openly laughing and waving.

She hasn't helped herself though. Yesterday I heard her boasting to a group of mums in the playground that she was 'schooling Alice's dressage horse for her after school as a favour.' A comment I would say she now regrets. I would also hazard a guess she wished she hadn't gone quite so to town with the rest of her stories, particularly telling them all that she was taught to show jump by none other than Ellen Whitaker after spending last winter hunting with her and her uncles (and a few other international show jumpers), as one does. You just couldn't make it up, or maybe you could.

APRIL

Thursday 8th April

I've been so busy getting ready for the Easter egg hunt this Sunday that I forgot to tell you about the breakfast in bed and queens for the morning after our Babylady version of Crufts. I will say one thing for our children — they are good losers. To recap, Martha, Edward and Charles were discovered to be cheating and so lost both competitions, meaning they had to make breakfast for Agatha, Margot, Nora and Etta. Then the cheaters had to treat the winners as queens for the morning.

I admit I did help with breakfast but the boys went out into the garden to pick some daffodils to decorate the tray and Martha made the toast and stirred the scrambled eggs. I managed to persuade the 'queens' to take breakfast at the table as it would be much more civilised so, as the four queens sat sipping orange juice and devouring their scrambled eggs and bacon with Penny who, although she wasn't strictly a queen as she didn't take part, joined in as did Henry who never misses out on bacon and eggs and a butcher's sausage at the weekend.

The boys and Martha then shovelled some cereal into themselves and disappeared up to the stables to carry out their first orders of the morning, to take over Nora and Margot's Saturday jobs filling haynets and refilling the water buckets at the stables, then giving Sausage and Porker their breakfasts. Thanks to Penny now sleeping through the night, I'd woken early and had already fed the horses who were now all out in the fields, happily munching the spring grass that seemed to have appeared almost overnight and had given the dogs a run in the meadow.

Henry had tended to the pups while I was helping cook breakfast so, apart from the general tidy-through we do every Saturday, which includes everyone stripping their beds and Nora and I remaking them all with fresh sheets, and the constant cycle of washing that needs to happen to maintain some order in a family of ten, we had the day to have fun and so Henry and I had already decided how we were going to spend it.

Now the weather was improving, it had been decided that we wanted to do some work to the gardens and so had planned a trip to a super-duper, all-singing and dancing garden centre about an hour from home. I used to love going to a garden centre when I was a kid. My kids didn't have the same enthusiasm.

'A garden centre! For God's sake, I don't want to go to a stupid *garden* centre!' moaned Margot.

'Mum, do we have to, really?' asked Martha.

'I want to build dens with Charles!' said an outraged

Edward and on it went. Garden centres were crap; flowers were boring; I was boring, as was Henry.

'It will be fun. We need to get some bark, some flowers for the borders, a new wheelbarrow and a new BBQ,' I told them.

'Kill me now,' said Martha sarcastically.

'Oh, don't start, Martha. You'll have a good time and, if you're all good, we can have a jacket potato or a sandwich and a cake in the coffee shop!' said Henry desperately. After the usual debate of who was coming with me in my car and who went with Henry, we arrived at the garden centre which was bloody massive.

'Right, Penny and Charles, you can sit in the trolley. Agatha and Etta, you come and sit on this flat one here and I'll push you,' said Henry, taking one look at the packed car park and the size of the shop. Apart from Henry having to constantly shout at Martha to get her head out of her phone and look where she was going (after her almost knocking into a builder reading the back of a power-tool box and then walking smack bang into a display of discount house plants), and having to remind the rest of the girls that display trampolines are just that — display — which didn't extend to them each taking turns to do back flips while asking speechless staff members to mark them out of ten, it wasn't too bad until Penny had a screaming fit after spotting a purple watering can with a sunflower nozzle which she instantly decided she had to have in her life.

Henry and I looked at each other and came to a unanimous decision that it would be eight quid well spent if it kept her quiet the whole way around the aisles and, as Henry pointed out, hopefully by the time we were ready to leave she may have fallen out of love with it so we could casually discard it on a random shelf or, worst case scenario, offer to swap it for a Mars Bar from the sweet shelf at the tills.

Little did we know Charles was about to set his eyes on something that he wouldn't be willing to swap for a chocolate bar at the checkout. It was our own fault really. You would think with eight children we would have known better. We had just come out of the café and were heading to the tills when Etta spotted the pets corner.

'Look, there are animals!' she announced.

'Can we have a look please?' asked Edward.

Henry agreed we could have a look around before we left. Penny was transfixed on the tropical fish while Etta and Agatha recoiled passing the snakes and lizards. Margot and Nora were talking to a parrot that didn't seem to be as talkative as the sign and price tag suggested. Martha had little interest and sat on the floor, looking at her phone. *Hang on, where are Henry, Edward and Charles?* I thought. I rounded up the rest of the children and we went to look for them.

As we turned the corner and walked down the next aisle, I spotted Henry standing with Charles who was holding something orange and fluffy.

'Mummy! Look, it's a guinea pig! I've called him Norman!' I looked at Henry and rolled my eyes. He laughed and shrugged his shoulders and said, 'We'd better find him a house then.'

'And a friend. Guinea pigs are socially advanced animals. Norman could become sad alone, he needs a pal,' Charles informed us.

Of course he does, I thought. We ended up leaving the garden centre with a few things we went for as well as an overpriced watering can, a ginger guinea pig called Norman, and a very sweet, lop-eared rabbit who Norman has since seemingly decided was created for the sole purpose of being his naughty time plaything and now spends most of his day attempting to hump her while squeaking frantically like he does when Agatha (who, as pure as her intentions are, does have an unfortunate tendency to love little animals a tad too much) cuddles him and gives him a 'snuggle squeeze'.

His frantic bonking attempts haven't gone unnoticed by the younger children who think they're the funniest thing ever and have triggered some pretty cringeworthy story writing in the children's weekend school diaries together with detailed pictures and captions like 'Norman loves to ride my rabbit so much, he squeaks with joy!'

Evening

I just told Henry he's going to have to take the guinea pig to the vet when we get back from Cornwall to have his 'urges taken care of'. Henry got confused for a moment and pulled a disgusted face and said, 'There is no way I'm doing that! I can't believe you want me to ask the vet to wank off Norman!'

When I'd stopped laughing, I explained to Henry that I

meant for him to take Norman to be neutered, not for a hand job.

Saturday 10th April

Morning

Easter egg hunt tomorrow. I've taken the easy option and paid for three children's entertainers to run it. They bring all the props and clues then act all enthusiastic and take charge of the little people while dressed as Disney characters and, as the last head count including siblings and our friends' children was close to 85 kids, it's going to be money well spent. As well as all the children's school friends, we also have Florence and Adam, Beryl and Clive, Quinn and Richard and a few more of our friends coming.

The hog roast and bar have already been delivered and set up and the bouncy castle people are outside now inflating it while Daisy and Nancy stand in front of the children staring at them like they're about to be invaded. I feel like we've had the girlies for so long now. They've settled into our family so well, sleeping in the children's rooms every night now and following them around the grounds when they're outside. They're trustworthy around strangers but uninterested as they're very family orientated.

Evening

Wondering what to wear tomorrow. I texted and asked Florence who suggested 'smart casual'. What the fuck does that even mean though? I might just wear skinny jeans and a white Zara top with flats...Is that just casual though? Not sure who to ask...I can't ask Fiona as she only owns power suits and pencil skirts these days and Sarah seems to always wear Boden. Beth, who is my usual go-to, is away with Mario on a 'second honeymoon'. I could always ask Beryl I suppose, she has been much friendlier lately and has done a lot of hosting. Yes, I will ring Beryl.

'Oh, hello Beryl. It's Alice. I'm stuck on what to wear tomorrow. What do you think?' I asked her, holding the phone in one hand and opening a packet of biscuits to bribe the children into silence with the other.

'Well, something that fits for a start!' she scoffed.

'Yes, thanks, I mean what style would you go for?' I persevered.

'Well, you're representing your family and your home on a Sunday so I would suggest a blouse, simple pearls, a knee-length skirt and opaque tights.' She spoke slowly, like she was speaking to an idiot and answering the most obvious thing in the world.

'I thought, as we're outside, I could wear that Bretton stripe I have and some flats and jeans.'

'No, no, no! Jeans will simply not do! If you insist on trousers, at least wear some smart ones; ones that need ironing before you wear them. Have you considered the mustard dress you wore at Christmas? It's a little on the short side but it *is* a classic design and you could pair that with some black tights and boots. That would be a passable outfit,' Beryl said, which was more a statement than a question but it was actually a very good idea.

Sunday 11th April

I wore the dress. Everyone said I looked nice, apart from Beryl who said it wasn't as flattering as she remembered it to be. The party was brilliant. All the children had an amazing time, bouncing on the castle, scoffing Easter eggs they'd found on the hunt. The party entertainers were worth their weight in gold; I have no idea where they get their energy from. All afternoon they floated around dressed as various Disney princesses, singing *Frozen* songs, face painting everyone and playing endless games. The pony rides were a huge hit too.

The food seemed to go down well and the bar possibly a bit too well. Henry invited Ian who, despite bringing his girlfriend, was on top knobhead form after a few vodka, lime and sodas and, after abandoning his girlfriend talking to a group of mums from the school, he swaggered over and plotted himself up by the hog roast (which was, thank God, a child-free zone), where he stood cockily asking every female, 'Do you want some hot sauce with that?' while winking and pairing up his leer with a far-from-subtle hip-thrusting gesture.

He met his match however when his vodka-based bravery reared its head once again and pushed him to try his chat-up line and hip movements out on Florence who looked at him like he was something the cat had dragged in. 'There are children on the premises, you disgusting little man,' she sneered, 'and may I remind you I've seen your sauce provider many times before thanks to the powers of Facebook so I know as well as you do, that ridiculous thrusting and sexual advances implying you have the kit to live up to your offerings is both misleading and very pathetic!'

I could tell by his blood-shot eyes and his swaying body as he shrugged his shoulders that Ian was more than just a bit pissed; he was, in fact, super pissed and, I predicted, going to be his usual dick-like self. Proving me right he slapped Florence on the arse and then turned to Adam, who had appeared to retrieve his pork bap from Florence, and shouted, 'She fucking loves it really! I reckon she is such a dirty bitch behind closed doors. Am I right, Adam, does she love it?!' which, although was very disrespectful, I have to admit I did find really funny, mainly because of Florence's face.

'I will leave you to deal with this disgusting pervert, Adam. *Do not* let me down!' said an outraged Florence who then stormed off with her head held high, leaving Adam rooted to the spot in anger and me apologising to the small crowd of guests looking on, seemingly eagerly awaiting Adam's response.

All things considered, Adam was very controlled and, after taking a deep breath, he strode over to Ian and dragged him very roughly aside by his shirt collar and thundered, 'I am going to give you a word of advice, lad. Lay off the sauce and do not *ever* call my wife a dirty bitch again or I shall have no choice but to chin you! DO YOU UNDERSTAND ME, YOU LITTLE BASTARD? I WILL DROP YOU!' which caused tears of laughter to run down my cheeks.

Ian, despite puffing out his shoulders and muttering as he walked away that he 'wasn't bothered' and was 'hard as fuck and would take on anyone', disappeared pretty much straight after and wasn't found until Henry went to check on the puppies a few hours later and discovered Ian 'I will take you all on' fast asleep on a pallet of pig feed, clutching a half-eaten Easter egg smeared in what looked like apple sauce.

Tuesday 13th April

Martha and Margot have no taste in books! While Henry was rummaging in the loft searching for our suitcases, I managed to persuade him to dig out my original copies of Ruby Ferguson's *Jill* series for the girls to read at bedtime.

I was so excited, expecting them to gush about how great they were but, instead, they looked at them with disinterest and reluctantly agreed to start reading the first book, *Jill's Gymkhana*. Twenty minutes after going up, they came back down with the whole series in their arms and dropped them on the kitchen table and said they didn't want to read them due to them being 'weird and crap'.

This seriously enraged me. I'm sure anyone who has read these books would feel the same. Jill is neither weird nor crap.

'What do you mean, crap? These are the best books I've ever read!' I exclaimed.

'Erm, Mum, we don't even understand what the girl is going on about. I mean, what language are they? She talks so funny in it and she seems a bit of a drip to be honest with you.'

'Language? What do you mean, what language? It's English of course, and they're all about ponies...You love ponies and Jill is not a drip!' I insisted, thinking I was beginning to sound a bit desperate.

'I think they're just a bit too old-fashioned for us, Mum. Sorry we don't want to read them. Thanks anyway though,' said Martha in a slightly patronising tone.

What has the world become? I feel really sad they've rejected them to be honest. I might try to force them on Nora instead; failing that, Etta and Agatha who are much broader minded in their reading material. I read them both some real-life stories from a *Woman's Weekly* in the dentist last week to pass the time; didn't hear *them* complaining.

Monday 19th April

10 a.m.

All the puppies left over the weekend for new homes. Despite knowing they each have a happy life ahead of them, we'll miss them all hugely. It was very much bittersweet. Still, we're off to Cornwall today for a week, driving both cars and dividing four dogs and eight children between us. God give me strength. This is going to be one fucking awful journey. Quinn and Robert hun (Mr Plait) have agreed to come and feed and water the horses, pigs and The MIL (cat, not the human one). Robert is actually a good horseman as he grew up looking after his dad's heavyweight cob who, by all accounts, was a bit of a brute.

11 p.m.

We had all the cars packed before breakfast and were '100% leaving before midday'. At ten past two, we finally started our journey. I'm now debating if it would be in any way possible to just stay in Cornwall indefinitely in order to avoid having to get into the car with two dogs (Daisy and Nancy) who spent the whole journey here howling and barging the dog boot grill with their fat arses, trying to get into the back seat with the four children (Agatha, Penny, Edward and Margot) who spent the whole time kicking my seat, arguing over what to watch on their iPad, announcing they were hungry, needing a wee, feeling sick, wanted to get out, hated car journeys, repeatedly asking me if I knew where I was going and if I had enough petrol, all of which contributed to making me want to lose the will to live and mutter, 'FMFL,' constantly for the last two hours of the journey.

Henry as usual fared much better than me. After he listened to my account of 'the drive from hell', he pulled a patronising face and said that his journey was 'great' despite him also having two dogs (Chubb and Tara) who slept the whole way and four children (Charles, Martha, Nora and Etta) who passed him snacks, repeated what the sat nav said if he didn't hear it, didn't kick the seats once and were actually 'excellent company and no bother at all'. Smug fucker.

Wednesday 21st April

We are having a lovely time. The house is a stereotypical Cornwall holiday home, painted bright white with stone floors and signs on the wall with quotes like 'seaside life is the best life' and shells decorating every possible surface. It's right on the beach and the children have spent most of their time since we arrived paddling and playing with buckets and spades. Even Martha, once she had got over the lack of Wi-Fi access, has been joining in.

We had one incident involving Edward who decided to draw a ring in the sand using a stick then smacked Charles down face first into the sand WWE style, winding him quite badly, but, other than that, it's been fairly stress free.

The dogs have a big enclosed garden area so they've been no trouble. Beryl has been the most pleasant surprise of all. She has been nice to me. Well, not nice exactly, but she has directed her moaning more towards Henry so far, having brought up his pal Ian as 'the weak link in your circle, son' several times, but she hasn't really made any digs or comments directed at me at all.

It's actually been very relaxed so far. We're having a BBQ this evening which Clive and Henry have taken charge of. Why is it that, all year, most men can't even make themselves a sandwich without asking a hundred questions or calling for backup but, as soon as a BBQ is on the agenda, they all reinvent themselves as Gordon Ramsay. Henry actually tried to tell Beryl how to make chicken kebab this afternoon. He backed off when she jabbed him in the chest with her metal prongs and said, 'I have forgotten more about meal preparation than you will ever know so kindly piss off!'

Friday 23rd April

Evening

You know the saying 'ignorance is bliss'? Well, it's true. This evening I had gone upstairs to get Penny a pair of slippers as it's quite chilly in the evenings being so close to the sea and I overheard Beryl on the phone.

'One just has to make the best of it, Shirley. I have said it from day one. I couldn't stand her then and I can't stand her now but, for my son's sake, I have put up with her on this holiday. But you know how I feel. It just isn't good enough for my Henry. It never has been but he's made his bed with it and so what can one do?' she said in a martyred tone.

It?! Did she just call me 'it'?!

I know I said I wasn't going to take anything Beryl said to

heart anymore but I do feel like I've been punched in the stomach slightly. I haven't said anything to Henry. I don't want an atmosphere around the children. I'm not even sure I will tell him at all. I feel too embarrassed.

Sunday 25th April

I haven't said anything. Beryl tried to speak to me today and called me sweetie. Two-faced cow. We had a nice day though. We went to Monkey Sanctuary which Charles loved more than the rest of the children put together, although even he was a bit put out when the keeper wouldn't let him in the enclosure with them. Had fish and chips for supper. We wanted to get normal fish and chips wrapped in paper and sit on the beach but Queen Beryl wouldn't hear of it and insisted we eat at a celebrity chef's fish shop that charges you £5 as you walk through the door just for them allowing you to breathe the same air as them, then stand in a line to order your meal and sit in a non-air-conditioned, diner-type booth next to their fryers.

When we finally got to the front of the line, which seemed to take forever, especially since Agatha had decided to repeatedly ask us all what we were having and, if we said fish, what type of fish and so on, the server said, 'Hello.'

Agatha, who is always very chatty and friendly said, 'Hi! My name's Agatha and that's my grandma and, guess what? She loves cod!' Unfortunately for Beryl, who Agatha was pointing at, the sentence sounded less like 'she loves cod' and much more like 'she loves cock!'

The server looked down over the counter at Agatha. 'Sorry, maid, I've got an old set of ears. You're going to have to speak louder.'

I think, going by his smirk, he heard only too well the first time, as did the laughing crowd of diners. Agatha, who has never been a shy child, ignored the many customers and happily obliged the server's request and bellowed as loudly as she could while pointing at Beryl, 'I SAID, YOU SEE MY GRANDMA OVER THERE? SHE LOVES COCK!'

As the restaurant burst into laughter, I couldn't resist turning to Beryl and saying, 'No, Agatha. You see grandma doesn't really like it *"but one just has to make the best of it."'* Safe to say Beryl and I are now firmly on the same page and Agatha is now my favourite child.

Tuesday 27th April

Home sweet home. So glad to be back. Quinn left me a note detailing how he couldn't be here to greet us because he'd gone for a tetanus jab as my 'insane, demonic fluffball' ambushed him from on top of the fridge freezer, jumping onto his back and biting his ear 'like a feline Hannibal'. Was glad to hear that us being away hasn't affected The MIL's mental health.

MAY

Sunday 3rd May

Evening

Badminton Horse Trials. We had a family day out today for my birthday. Penny set the tone with her epic tantrum over her outfit. I had got all the girls white shorts and Joules polo shirts and the boys the same but in royal blue. Penny was having none of it.

'Not wearing it,' was her reply when I said it was time to get dressed.

'Come on, everyone has new clothes. Put yours on and we can go to watch the horses and have a picnic,' I pleaded.

'No, I want best outfit!'

'Fucking brilliant,' I muttered under my breath.

'Best outfit' started as a dressing-up outfit which then developed into wear-at-home outfit, which then snuck into wearing-to-the-shops attire, and now, given the chance, she would wear it all day every day. This isn't ideal as 'best outfit' is a bright pink ball gown/bridesmaid dress which started its life with Martha; a pair of polka-dot wellies which she took a likening to from Etta's wet play school bag that are several sizes too big; and an adult-sized, purple, sparkly baseball cap embossed with 'Malia Rocks!' which I ordered for Fiona for her upcoming holiday, not because I thought she would wear it, but because I am a piss taker by nature and was most disappointed when Penny spotted it and refused to give it back to me. An hour later I had attempted to dress her countless times, which she objected to and threw herself on the living room rug and screamed and screamed.

'We need to get everyone in the car,' said Henry, putting his head around the door.

'I don't know what to do with her. She's refusing to get dressed and I can't force her. She started shouting, "Help me, help me, Childline," when I tried to put her shorts on her a minute ago,' I said.

Henry laughed. 'You go and get in the car. Leave this one to me. I'll have her dressed in the outfit you've chosen for her and out to the car in five minutes.'

'You won't!' said a defiant Penny.

'Five minutes, darling,' said a confident, borderline-smug Henry, gesturing to the door.

Fifteen minutes later I saw movement coming out of the front door. Henry came out stern-faced followed by Penny who floated out in her ballgown, wellies and her Malia Rocks baseball cap. She was beaming in triumph, waving to her waiting siblings. I gave Henry a look as he got into the car. 'I decided that it's a fairly sensible outfit, given the wellies and the cap, so I thought I would let her wear it to keep her happy after all,' he said straight-faced.

'She wouldn't get dressed for you either then?' I asked, chuckling.

'No, the little madam bit my hand before I even got her socks on then threw the Sky remote at my head,' he said, shaking his head.

At least we were on our way. Martha and Margot sat glued to their iPads while the little ones repeatedly asked me 'are we nearly there yet?' every five minutes from leaving the end of our driveway.

We had arranged to meet Florence, Adam, Beth and Mario at the entrance. We hadn't seen Beth and Mario since the situation, which wasn't to be spoken of again ('the situation' being Mario is a cheating bastard), so I was hoping it wouldn't be awkward. After a few phone calls, we all found each other. Henry, who has zero interest in horses, opted to take Charles, Edward and Penny (who was getting some very strange looks in her buggy thanks to her style choices) to look around the other stalls with Mario and Adam, while I took the rest of the girls who, as you know, are horse mad, with Florence and Beth.

Florence was child-free as her children were away with Adam's family for the weekend so, knowing my children like she does and their tendency to wander, she took charge of Agatha and Etta which was the best birthday present I could have wished for.

Beth was her normal self and we didn't mention Mario, which was just what I hoped for. We decided to have a walk around the cross-country course. The children were bursting to see the eventers take the leap over the water jump so we had a long slow walk there and joined the vast crowd who had the same idea as us. Before long we had managed to get to a good vantage point and were able to watch horses and their riders successfully coordinate the complex water element with style, and commiserate with those who weren't so lucky.

We all enjoyed every second and, what seemed like only a few minutes later but in fact was a few hours, Adam called Florence and asked us to meet them over at the Lakeside Pavilion.

Henry surprised me by renting a marquee, complete with a closed-circuit television showing all the action across country, and set out all our picnics. I felt so spoiled. The marquee had a picket-fenced garden area which looked onto the breath-taking Badminton lake and was decked out with comfy furniture. In the centre was a table covered with flowers and a beautiful birthday cake decorated with dusky pink sugar peonies.

'Happy birthday, darling,' said Henry, giving me a kiss.

'We men will be driving this evening so you girls can have an afternoon off,' added Adam, which caused Florence to look at him like he was from outer space.

She turned to me and whispered, 'Well, this is a turn-up

for the books. If I find out Adam's having an affair, I will cut his bollocks off.'

I laughed but Beth didn't.

Little did I know that was the start of the day going downhill. We were all getting on well, as normal, but I noticed Florence and Beth had been a bit off with each other. The children had a brilliant afternoon, happily watching the closed-circuit TV and doing handstands and cartwheels along the lawns, demolishing my delicious birthday cake with forks. By early evening Henry and co decided to get some ice creams with all the children before we left for home so off they all went apart from Penny who was sleeping in her buggy with her Yanit after finally being prised out of her 'best outfit' and into some fresh cotton PJs that I'd packed for all the little people to change into before we headed home.

Florence and Beth, being child free, had drunk several bottles of wine by this point. I wasn't drinking so I noticed a bit of tension between them both again, which was very unlike them.

'It was lovely of Henry to arrange this, wasn't it? I wonder what he's after!' said Beth jokingly.

'Not every husband only does nice things for their wife through a guilty conscience, darling,' said Florence.

Here we bloody go, I thought, rolling my eyes and trying to change the subject.

'And what is that supposed to mean then?' asked Beth as she put her glass down, glaring at Florence.

'I mean what I say. Don't tar our husbands with your husband's brush!' slurred Florence.

'My husband's brush? What's that you're saying? I suppose Adam is perfect then, is he? Is that what you're saying?' thundered Beth who had stood up from her seat with her hand on her hip.

'That's enough! Stop it, both of you!' I said, sensing it could get heated. I was again ignored and Florence continued.

'That is exactly what I am saying, Beth, and given Adam who, unlike your husband, hasn't been in more knickers than she has changed nappies,' she spat, while pointing at me then standing up before continuing, 'yes, Beth, compared to your joke of a husband and marriage, indeed my husband and marriage are perfect. In fact, you are pathetic, a joke yourself, to tell you the truth!' ranted Florence at a now red-faced-with-fury Beth.

'STOP!' I shouted at them both. They continued to take no notice.

Beth then slapped Florence hard across the face and screamed, 'Get fucked, you stuck up tart and, by the way, you're right! Your upper arms do look like a severely battered minge!'

Florence gasped and retaliated by giving Beth a really hard shove on the back of the head as she leaned down to pick up her bag and cool box. Beth picked herself up off the ground and stormed off while I stood like a rabbit in the headlights, gobsmacked.

'Truth hurts!' bellowed Florence after Beth, before

storming off in the opposite direction.

Sunday 10th May

Morning

A week later and Beth and Florence still aren't talking. I'm quite pissed off they behaved like that on my birthday but I know drinking three bottles of wine and a jug of Pimm's probably didn't help the situation. I'm not getting involved. They've both phoned me since, mainly to slag off the other one, but I'm staying well out of it and have told them both not to discuss it with me. In honesty I agree with Florence in what she said, but not the way she said it. She really shouldn't have said most of it at all though and Beth shouldn't have really said that Florence has upper arms like a severely battered minge.

8 p.m.

The school is coming in the morning in hourly slots then the pre-school are coming in the afternoon to use the pool. They've managed to fit the lessons all in one day to cut transport costs. The school kids are so excited. The PTA fund-raising is paying for a little mini bus each Monday from now to the end of the summer term to transport them all as it's too far to walk. Amanda, Clair and two class teachers are accompanying the children and assisting in the actual lessons. I've been demoted to the snack bitch and so have spent the evening cooking sausage rolls and making crustless finger sandwiches and mini pitta pizzas. I've also ordered two large glass Kilner tap jars to make fresh cordial and put sliced oranges in. Hope all goes well.

Monday 11th May

Swimming lessons. Huge success; the school was so well organised, they put swimming instructor Babs at our previous pool to shame. The school children looked so cute as they each arrived in their year groups, smiling and waving at me as they rushed off the bus and lined up, apart from my own children (with the exception of Agatha, Charles and Etta) who all ignored my waves and pretended they didn't know me.

Amanda and Clair emerged from the changing rooms looking like *Baywatch The Reunion*, both in matching, high-leg, bright red swimsuits that left nothing to the imagination, a sweat headband and a whistle around their necks.

Hats off to them though, they've given up all day every Monday from today until the end of the summer term. I can't really comment on the actual lessons as I left them to it other than delivering the snacks and drinks at the end as Penny is going through a really clingy stage and didn't want to stay inside with Henry. She's also at an age where she's savagely honest so I didn't want her around the Baywatch babes and the school teachers in their rather risqué Marks and Spencer two pieces. Not after what she said to me about my 'wobbly belly' and 'enormous boobies' when I was getting dressed this morning.

Saturday 16th May

Charles stinks and I can't work out why. He's had a shower and brushed his teeth and yet he still smells like death. I really can't work out where the smell is coming from. It's come on all of a sudden. I might have to take him to the doctor.

Evening

I worked out the mystery of the stinking kid. I turned to Google and stumbled across a Netmums thread. Basically the horrified woman in the thread described her son smelling like rotten meat and, after several visits to the dentist and the doctor, they discovered he had something up his nose which was causing the smell.

Henry had left for a few days away so this afternoon I called upon Martha for backup. 'Martha I need you to help me for a few minutes please. I think Charles has something stuck up his nose!'

'That's gross!' replied Martha, turning her nose up.

'Yes, I know but I want to have a look so I need you to hold the light for me.'

'For goodness' sake, okay then. I bet he has something there, he's always putting things up his nose. He's disgusting,' said Martha.

'Charles, come here please,' I called. My God, he did stink, poor boy. 'Right, Charles, have you got anything up your nose? I think you have and it's making you smell.'

Charles responded by shrugging his shoulders.

'Lie down and let me have a look,' I said, gesturing to the sofa.

As Charles was lying down, Nora came in. 'He probably has, you know. Him and Edward have competitions to see who can put stuff up there and blow it out the furthest!'

'Is that true, Charles? You know you shouldn't put things up your nose! It's very dangerous!'

No response. Sure enough, as I leaned down beside him and tilted his head back, using my phone torch I could clearly see something.

'For Christ's sake, Charles, there's something up your nose! Martha, get my tweezers. I think I can get it myself.'

Martha returned with my tweezers and I gently managed to capture it and pull the object out of Charles's nostril. It was a substantial piece of bath sponge and it bloody reeked.

'Why is there bath sponge up your nose?' I asked.

Charles, who clearly didn't know or care, replied, 'I can't remember. Can I go and see Norman now?'

Once the sponge was out, the smell disappeared almost immediately and, after a very stern talking-to and a few white lies about what could possibly happen if anything got badly stuck up a nose, I'm hopeful I won't have a repeat of it with him or any of the others anytime soon. I probably will though because they never listen.

Tuesday 19th May

6 p.m.

Just back from walking Daisy and Nancy which in itself is currently a major event. Martha pushes the buggy with Penny in it while Etta and Agatha ride their scooters and the rest of the gang ride their bikes. Henry and I take a dog each, usually one of two choices — Chubb who stops to wee on everything every five seconds or Tara who drags along behind or if it's the Mastiffs go you have two options-Nancy, who now weighs more than I do, has zero manners despite our constant training attempts and either plods along as unenthusiastically as possible until she spots someone or something exciting to which she then nearly pulls your arm out of its socket as she attempts (and usually succeeds) to drag you over to investigate, or Daisy who, to be fair, walks fairly well but then, like her sister, lets herself down when she spots someone or something new, but in a different way to Nancy.

Daisy's trademark is what the kids now call a 'Daisy Dive'. As soon as she spots someone new, she throws herself down by the feet of whoever is walking her and plays dead. She also sometimes pisses herself which has sometimes left the person walking her with wet feet. Due to me no longer being able to hold Nancy, that lucky person is always me. The Daisy Dive has also, on a few occasions, caused me to trip over the silly dog and land right on top of her. Luckily she's well-built and well-cushioned and so at least she makes a soft landing and I don't do her any damage.

Each evening the children ride the ponies while Henry and I walk Tara and Chubb. The circuit takes us about thirty minutes. The same circuit in the opposite direction with the children on bikes and us walking Daisy and Nancy currently takes us about an hour, sometimes more, depending on how many Daisy Dives we encounter and how long it takes us to coax her back to her feet thereafter. The simple solution would be to stop walking the dogs on a lead in the evening and just exercise them loose in our fields like we do each morning and them let them roam all day like they do already but I don't want dogs that I can't walk so we will keep persevering.

Character-wise you couldn't ask for better. Out of the farmhouse on walks, they are friendly but alert, looking for danger. Well, Nancy is anyway and they're accepting of welcomed new friends. They are gentle and kind to dogs we meet on walks, it's just the leads that are the issue at the moment. Nancy has been a lot better behaved in a harness on our last few walks though so watch this space.

I have more news on the dog front. As our female dogs have passed all their health checks, we've decided that, when they're mature, we'd like them both to have a litter of pups. Henry had toyed with the idea of getting a male and female puppy from different litters and blood lines when we were looking and he found a beautiful male pup the other side of the country but then, because we fell in love with the two girls, we decided against the boy Henry had found, despite him being gorgeous and my favourite colouring, a black-masked face with a dark sable body. We didn't feel it would be fair to him or our other animals to take on too much at once.

Now the girls are settled and we know we want to breed them, we decided to have a look online to see what studs are available in England. Just out of interest. Henry was having a browse online in the 'for sale and stud' section on the breed directory while I sat helping Edward with his homework when Henry beckoned me in an excited voice. 'Alice, come and have a look at this!' he said, pointing to his laptop. The advert was for a male Mastiff, the same breed as the girls, who looked very much like the puppy we were hoping to get back in January. You could tell from the advert he was a very loved dog and was looking for a new home due to genuine circumstances and through no fault of his own or his current owners.

Henry and I had a discussion. We hadn't set out to have another dog but there was something about William that made me compelled to find out more about him. He looked very different to our girls as their breed comes in many different colours and he was also smaller than them but almost the same age, give or take a few weeks.

'What do you think?' Henry asked me.

'He sounds and looks a lovely dog. Usually I'd be dubious and discard an older dog, particularly a male, but from the photos of him playing with lots of other dogs and being so well socialised, I think we should at least find out more,' I said, scrolling through William's photos. There were some of him with his dog walker and a group of doggy friends, all different breeds and sizes, one on a sofa snuggled up looking at the camera with his big dark eyes and several of him swimming in the sea. It's hard to explain but I felt so drawn to him.

Once the children were in bed and the house was quiet, I made the call. No answer. My heart sank, thinking he must have found a home. Despite my hatred of voicemails, I did something very out of character for me and left a message.

About twenty minutes later, I got a call back. 'Hello, I am Ella. I am just returning your call about William,' said the friendly voice.

'Oh, hello, thank you for getting back to me. I was really hoping you would,' I said, smiling and giving Henry a thumbs-up.

After a long conversation with Ella, I learned a lot about both her and her partner. I warmed to her instantly. For unavoidable reasons they have to move abroad and quite rightly don't feel it's fair putting William through such a long flight and a long stint in quarantine so, despite clearly adoring him, they've made the hard decision to find him a new home. Ella said they had mountains of calls and emails about him, most of which she had yet to return or hadn't felt right for William, but she said when she listened to my voicemail, she felt compelled to phone me. Things got even weirder when I mentioned how we almost got a male pup when we got our girls.

It turns out William is the pup we almost got! We know for certain as he was the last of the litter after being held back as his breeder had wanted to keep him. He was obviously meant to be a Babylady! Ella and Andrew are travelling several hours to meet us this weekend, to see our home and see if William gets on with our other dogs and our children. I can't wait.

Saturday 23rd May

10 a.m.

William is visiting today. I am so excited, I woke up at six and we've all been counting down the hours until they arrive since after breakfast. To try and pass the time, I took Agatha out on a little hack on Tinker this morning. She gives me heart failure every time and today was unfortunately no exception. The main problem is Agatha's current riding ability belief doesn't yet match her current actual riding ability. Four times today she tried to talk me into letting her off the lead rein, which just wasn't happening, not after last time when she was pottering around the garden on him and begged me to take off the lead rein, promising not to go faster than a walk.

I'd relented, knowing that Tinker will always do as little as possible and is more likely to stop and refuse to move than spook or tank off with her. All was fine for a while until I stood horrified as I witnessed Agatha with my own eyes deliberately nudge Tinker quite insistently into a begrudged half-hearted trot. Agatha then started to bob about like a buoy on rough seas, lost her balance and tumbled off sideways. She later claimed Tinker did it of his own accord but, having seen her sneaky little nudges and gentle kicks, I told her off for fibbing and demoted her back to the lead rein. I was very grateful to Tinker for being sensible with her and, when I saw he was kind enough to stand next to Agatha while she got up, felt a pang of guilt for calling him 'that fucking fat Shitland' the day before when he did his usual escape trick and broke out of the pony paddock and demolished the vegetable patch and shit on the patio. I gave him an extra scoop of carrots that evening purely to ease my own conscience because he really eats more than enough as it is.

7 p.m.

Ella and Andrew arrived just after lunch. We'd left our dogs inside. Quinn had offered to come and sit with the children so we could meet William first and then introduce him to the dogs and the children after. William leapt out of the car and trotted up to Henry and I, tail wagging. He is so much more puppy-like than Daisy and Nancy which is a good thing as our adult dogs seem to sense he is still a pup and took to him after only a few minutes. Daisy and Nancy took a bit more convincing. I think they felt more protective of their home than Chubb and Tara so barked at him and retreated behind our cars for a while but William showed how gentle and genuine he is by giving them space and not showing one ounce of aggression or dominance. The girls finally gave in and, before long, they were all charging around the garden together then, when worn out, they lay quietly together by the back doors.

We put the girls away and decided to bring out Martha and Margot to see what William made of them. I should say at this point it was clear to see William was still a puppy despite his size and was extremely obedient and very well socialised. I had no worries introducing him to our kids at all. As expected he was a perfect gent as he was slowly introduced to them. After a lengthy chat, Ella and Andrew decided they felt William was right for us, as did we. So he has stayed with us!

Much as we were all over the moon for William to stay behind with us, watching Ella and Andrew say goodbye to him was really upsetting. There were a lot of tears but we have agreed to stay in close contact with each other and keep them updated each week on how he settles in.

We are being sensible though for now. William is sleeping separately to the rest of the dogs and is only mixing with them and the children one at a time under the supervision of Henry or I, just until he gets to know and trust us fully and vice versa. He is an absolute angel though so far and has fitted straight in. He really is a true credit to Ella and Andrew. They genuinely love him and want the best for him and so we will be keeping in regular touch with them for the foreseeable future.

Wednesday 27th May

William is already part of the furniture. He sleeps on my

bed which, as Chubb and Tara always sleep in our day room by the fire in the winter or on the sofas in the hall during the warmer months and Daisy and Nancy always sleep in the children's rooms, hasn't put anyone's nose out of joint apart from Henry's. Henry does love William but he doesn't love William's tendency to bed hog and snore. He does snore quite loudly but he is so cuddly and handsome that I forgive him. Henry has threatened to start sleeping in the spare room if I don't start making William sleep on the floor in the kitchen. The spare room is in the attic and is quite draughty, even in summer. Hope Henry doesn't get too cold up there.

Thursday 28th May

7 a.m.

Fiona just phoned and asked if I want to meet her for lunch. Wasn't that keen on the idea because Fiona, although older than me, doesn't have children yet and so her idea of meeting for lunch is looking around the cool clothes shops, the type that play hip hop and have Kendall Jenner lookalike 'style advisors' who look at you with pity if you ask for a size 12. Last time I was in one of those shops and asked for a size 10, the shop assistant (sorry, 'style advisor') had the cheek to ask, 'Do you want to me to grab a 12 as well to save me going back to get it after?' It's comments just like that which have driven me to online shopping. Less judgement.

ALICE BABYLADY

Told Fiona I wasn't that keen because I had Penny, Agatha and Charles and that, as much as their table manners have improved, I didn't feel ready to take all three of them to the sort of place Fiona likes to lunch which is always a small, very quiet bistro that has lots of expensive glassware and judging by the last time we met in one, charges you fifteen quid for an 'open ham salad club' which is essentially one slice of seeded bread, a few leaves and some random green dodgy dip (possibly pesto dressing), a few slices of (admittedly good quality) ham and about five crisps. Wasn't impressed with it personally; if I'm paying fifteen quid for a sandwich, I want at the very least butter and two slices of bread and some chips and a good portion at that.

Fiona listened and agreed a bistro wasn't really a place for children, especially mine, then said, 'I know, we can go to Pizza Express. Lots of kids go there.'

I ummed and ahhed then suggested we perhaps went to Brewers Fayre as they have a ball pit.

'Good God, we aren't eating there! We aren't savages!' Fiona exclaimed, which I thought was a bit snobby but let it go as she didn't yet grasp the pull factor of Brewers Fayre. I agree the food isn't great but it offers free child care so will always be a winner in my book.

Reluctantly agreed to Pizza Express. Meeting at 1 p.m. It will take me an hour to get there so, if I start getting ready after I drop the girls and Edward off at holiday club (it's half term), I may just make it in time.

Evening

Not the best lunch to be honest. The leaving the house regime went fairly well apart from losing a ten-minute debate with Penny over her not wanting to wear a pull-up. She's at the stage where she doesn't wear one at home but I'm not confident she can go without on long car journeys and days out. Tried to persuade her to wear one 'just in case'. I was abruptly informed that she was 'a big girl now and didn't need one'.

I wasn't so confident but she wasn't budging and then she was so sure that she had it all under control, it was kind of infectious. Agatha also put her thoughts into the mix, tutting at me and announcing that, 'Penny is fine in knickers.'

'Ummm,' I found myself saying. 'Okay then but you must tell Mummy if you need the toilet, Penny. Okay?' What a knob I am.

We arrived in good time, no arguments en route which was a welcome miracle. I buggied up Penny in her seat one side and tried to get Charles to sit the other. Agatha, who despite being younger, is much bigger and much faster at walking than him, held onto the buggy instead. Charles took huge exception to this and folded his arms and refused to stand on the buggy board or sit in the buggy. FFS. Not wanting him to start a full-on tantrum, I backed down.

'Right, fine, just hold the buggy then,' which somehow then triggered an argument between him and Agatha over who was standing which side. At this point I resorted to bribing them both with a box of Tic Tacs which, after the incident with Etta getting one stuck up her nose the other year, always makes me shudder in fear of a repeat but desperate times call for risk and so I poured a handful into each of their chubby palms and finally left the car park.

The lack of pull-up was on my mind so I asked Penny about ten times to 'try for a toilet' as we passed Gregg's. Yes, I'm one of those annoying people who use Gregg's as a public toilet although on this occasion I did buy twelve jam doughnuts for everyone to have at home later. I then spent ten minutes standing outside New Look, the meeting place, telling Charles and Agatha reasons why we shouldn't feed seagulls or pigeons and cursing Fiona for being late (as usual).

Ten minutes or so later, she finally glided towards us, looking polished and preened in a cream suit which is a look that only women who do not have to endure two hours of leaving the house child dramas or little people with chocolate-covered sticky hands can pull off.

In all honesty I was a bit put out that, as always, I was on time despite having children with me and was left waiting. My irritation was all soon forgotten though. As predicted, Fiona wanted to have a look around the shops before lunch and made a predictable beeline for the Kendall Jenner shops which today went quite well. The little ones had a dance to Kanye West while Fiona debated whether she needed any more hot pants for her upcoming Malia jaunt. Having finally decided to get two pairs, she announced she needed to stock up on fake tan so she's 'beach ready from touchdown' so we had to head to Boots.

While Fiona pondered which brand to go for, I decided I was feeling a bit left out so basketed a bottle of St. Moriz Darker Than Dark and an applicator mitt. Penny spotted a back loofah; at least, I think that's what it was. Anyway, whatever it was, she wanted it. I was debating just buying it to pacify her until I noticed the £18 price tag. *Eighteen quid for a loofah on a stick! Boots can jog on. I'll take the tantrum and threats to remove all her clothes for the best part of twenty quid.* I told her kindly but firmly 'no' and was baffled when she took it well and didn't threaten to bite herself or to take her shoes and tights off and throw them. Phew.

'Shall we head to Pizza Express now?' I asked, not wanting to push my luck.

'Yes, okay, I'm starving,' Fiona agreed.

When we arrived at Pizza Express, it was busy but thankfully the staff put us in the far corner. I seated Agatha and Charles either side of me by the wall so they couldn't run off. Penny was in a high chair and I was ashamed to say I became a bit smug at this point. *What was I worried about?* I thought. *This is fine.* I make a mental note to do this more often. Before long the food arrived — pizza, garlic bread and dough balls. Charles started to moan about the lack of fries but soon settled for the pizza and a sip of Fiona's coke.

Then it happened. Agatha was first to mention it.

'Mummy, what's that smell?'

Oh God, no. Shit. Literally.

Penny then confirmed. 'That's me, Ags. I'm pooing and I can't stop it,' she said, laughing.

Fiona instantly put down her fork and looked at me. Her face was just one of sheer horror. I laughed because, in all honesty, it was so dire it was a laugh or cry moment.

The running commentary didn't stop there. I tried to zone out for a few seconds to think what I was going to do. So much for not needing pull-ups. A few people looked around. *Oh God, I thought, I really need to get Agatha and Penny to stop talking about shit in the middle of Pizza Express.*

In my calmest mummy voice, I said, 'That's enough. Please be quiet; people are trying to eat,' with a look that said 'shut up now'.

Agatha being Agatha took no notice whatsoever and carried on asking Penny various graphic, shit-related questions while Charles continued to much on his garlic bread obliviously.

'Penny, can you walk to the toilet with Mummy?' I asked hopefully.

Penny shook her head. 'No, Mum, I have poo all down my legs.'

'Ok, darling,' I said, still in my upbeat mummy voice. Fucking fabulous. Fiona had still yet to say anything. Instead she was frozen to the spot, completely and utterly horrified.

'Fi, you're going to have watch these two while I take Penny into the toilet.' I said, gesturing to Agatha and Charles, then leaning down to rummage in the buggy, I then realised I was so caught up in the 'I don't need a pull-up' speech that I'd packed the wrong clothes pile and the spare trousers and top I had were Charles's not Penny's. *Great*, I thought to myself, *she'll kick off now about having to wear boy's clothes.*

The restaurant was still heaving and the toilet was right on the other side of the packed-out room. I decided it was a now or never situation so scooped Penny up in a sort of fireman's lift while holding her at arm's length. Armed with baby wipes and Charles's clean clothes, I hurried across to the toilets as stealthily as possible which isn't at all possible when carrying a poo-covered and stinky child over your shoulder. I got a few sympathetic glances and nods and finally reached the disabled loo.

I could still hear Agatha bellowing, 'My sister has done a massive poo and she's got no knicker nappy on! Her name's Penny Babylady and she likes Topsy and Tim,' followed by a desperate-sounding Fiona.

'Agatha, sweetie, please can you sit down for Auntie Fiona? There's a good girl. Stop talking about Penny. If you sit down, Auntie Fiona will give you her phone to play with or money! Do you want some money?'

Agatha didn't seem to take Fiona up on her offers of an iPhone or hush money and instead carried on with graphic toilet-based over-sharing. Oh, for God's sake.

Meanwhile I was still debating what to do with Penny. It was pretty fucking bad; like shoulders to ankles bad. I decided I was going to have to strip her off and just put the clothes in a nappy bag and clean her with baby wipes. I have to say, at that point, Penny really didn't seem to care at all. In fact I think she was actually enjoying it. I took a deep breath and started stripping her off, dumping the clothes in nappy sacks. The smell was absolutely awful. I then used a whole packet of baby wipes to clean her as best as I could.

Worst part over. As I was washing my hands, I told her she needed to put a pull-up on and she agreed. Then she spotted the clothes — a blue pair of cords and a dinosaur top. After eyeing them she scrunched up her face and shouted, 'Not my clothes! They're brothers! I NOT wear those!'

FFS.

I attempted to explain that that's all we had and could she please just pop them on and we'd go straight to the car then go home, have a bath and put her own fresh clothes on.

I got glared at and given a very stern 'NO!' which is basically a toddler version of saying 'get fucked'.

I had no choice then but to pull out the big guns.

'Penny, if you wear your brother's clothes, when we get home I will give you some of my Lindt chocolates.'

Her answer was still, 'NO!'

I was feeling the pressure as I could still hear Agatha who seemed to have now coaxed Charles into the poo conversation.

'Okay, if you get dressed right now, I'll give you all the Lindt chocolates and a can of coke.'

That got her attention.

'Red one?' she questioned but it was clear from her face the question was more of a proposition. She may be a toddler but she knew I knew that was the deal breaker and, as I was in a toilet surrounded by bags of shit and the only way out was her getting her in Charles's clothes, I took the offer on the table.

'Yes, OK, the red one.'

She laughed and said, 'Okay, mummy. I love dinosaurs and blue trousers. I was going to wear them anyway.'

Of course you were.

A few minutes later, dressed like a boy and smelling like a mixture of my perfume (which I had doused her in) and Dettol hand wipes, Penny strutted out of the toilet, loudly declaring that she was 'all clean now' then offering more details than needed such as, 'My mum has my clothes in bags and they have poo on them.' She got applause and a cheer from a group of men in suits.

We got back to the table to a shell-shocked Fiona. Not sure if it was due to me making her check if there was poo on Penny's T-shirt before we left the table (which there was) or being left in charge of Agatha the fog horn, but either way she was stressed and it was time to go. To be fair to Pizza Express, the staff were lovely and packed up all our food in little boxes and containers, probably hoping we would leave before someone else 'had a very bad accident' as Agatha kept saying.

Three hours after leaving the house, I was back home with some cold pizza and a smug Penny who was still wearing a green dinosaur top while guzzling a can of coke and smelling faintly of shit and perfume waiting for her bath to run.

I suspect I now have a 30-year old friend who wants to be

sterilised.

JUNE

Tuesday 2nd June

3 p.m.

Beth and Florence are speaking again thank goodness. They met for supper and, while neither would apologise, Sarah, who was there as mediator, made them see sense and they have both agreed to draw a line and move forward. I am so pleased.

Evening

Just sent Ella and Andrew a text and photos of William standing with the children in the garden and one of him asleep on my bed. I love him so much; he also loves cheese as much as I do. I believe he is my spiritual animal.

Friday 5th June

Evening

It's Martha's birthday tomorrow. She has hit the stroppy, pre-teen stage in the last few months and has been quite hard work. We've hired a glamping bell tent to be set up in the garden in the morning for a girly sleepover. Apart from providing snacks and ordering takeaway, I'll leave them all to it which, from what I can gather, is the best gift for an eleven-year-old. It all sounded simple but the build-up has been a real headache. Mainly due to schoolgirl politics.

Martha's class is very small and there are only five girls and Martha and, for whatever reason, she hasn't taken to one of the girls and vice versa, so didn't want to invite that one girl which, in my eyes, just wasn't an option. I strongly disagree with leaving children out especially in such a small group and so I basically said she was to invite her with a good heart because, although they don't get on, they haven't actually been horrible to each other.

Martha agreed I was right and that she would invite her and say she hoped she would come. The girl has accepted the invitation and they seem to be making more of an effort with each other now. Martha is currently in the village at the girl's house so I'm pleased they've managed to find some kind of friendship. I know from my own experience with Amanda that first impressions can be deceptive; we get on well now.

Saturday 6th June

1 p.m.

The glamping company have done a marvellous job. The bell tent is huge. We had them put it up right at the bottom of the garden so the girls are in view but feel they have privacy. The tent looks stunning — a cream fabric with grass-reed carpet. It's decorated so beautifully, very girly and boho.

I've laid out matching PJs and slippers on each airbed together with a pamper pack. Electric candles are placed on top of little bedside tables at the side of each bed and scatter cushions have been stacked up in the centre for them to lounge on. Henry has rigged up a safety outdoor extension lead and set up a small television and DVD player so they can watch DVDs and, next to it, I've left a snack basket full of sweets, popcorn and drinks. Outside, the tent is decorated with bunting, twinkly fairy lights and candle lanterns. I've hung paper pompoms in the trees and life-size flamingos are standing each side of the tent.

Martha is chuffed with it. I think my main issue is keeping the rest of the little Babyladys away from it.

11 p.m.

I've been running around like a headless chicken since the girls arrived at 4 p.m. It's been worth it however as it's all been great. The girls went swimming then sat around the pool eating burgers. Martha, bless her, invited all her sisters out to the tent for the evening to watch films and share the snacks with her which I thought was really sweet of her. No one really wants their younger sisters tagging along, do they? Anyway, they went out there for an hour or so then slowly drifted back in and by seven all the girls were back inside and Martha and her friends have been left in peace since. Groups of girls can sometimes be silly but they've been really sensible and well behaved.

Sunday 7th June

11 a.m.

The party guests have just left after all sitting down with us for a cooked breakfast. A few of the girls were so thrilled to go with Margot and Martha to collect the eggs this morning and feed the pigs. I always presume because we're all so rural here that all the children are living like mine are but it seems not. One of Martha's friends asked me if it was definitely safe to eat our chickens' eggs as they didn't have a use-by date on them.

Evening

Spent the afternoon gardening while the children argued who was in charge of the tent; an argument which was predictably won by Agatha and Etta as they always scream the loudest. The boys had to have their Nerf guns taken off them after they shot me on the bum one too many times. Those things look innocent enough but the pellets have a right sting to them, especially when you're not expecting it.

The farmhouse is almost back to its best. The orchards and fruit trees have all been cleared and pruned and the wisteria that smothers the whole of the farmhouse frontage is in full bloom; the buds are so vast and substantial. Some of the bigger stems are almost buckling under the weight of the deep purple flowers. The pond is also full of life, flowering water lilies are sprinkled all over its surface, a palette of pinks and yellows, and the lush green reeds are currently playing house to a family of ducklings which bring Charles hours upon hours of pleasure watching them go about their day.

The pigs are growing like weeds and now come to call and our chicken family has grown from four to sixteen. They are happy little clucks, as I call them and have been rewarding us for their new coop and fox-proof garden with an abundance of eggs. Sometimes, dare I say, even for a family of ten, at times we have too many and I run out of ways to use them all. Not that I'm complaining. Life is good.

Friday 12th June

5 p.m.

I have orange umpa lumpa children. Etta and Margot decided they were looking a bit too pasty and so helped themselves to my St Moriz Darker Than Dark self-tan. When asked why they did it, Margot sheepishly said, 'Sorry, Mum, we just wanted to look like the TOWIE girls and so we put a bit on, then a bit more, then some more to even it up and then…well…things just got really out of hand.'

We're supposed to be going for a day out to a safari park tomorrow so now we either have to cancel or take two kids who look like the *Bargain Hunt* presenter. I might try washing them in lemon juice; it may tone down the soggy-biscuit smell if nothing else.

Saturday 13th June

Evening

Went to the safari park. Etta and Margot still look like they've been Tango'd. Several people giggled at them and made comments as they passed them. Usually along the lines of, 'Oh, deary me!'

One woman, who looked a lot like Denise from *The Royle Family* TV program who was wearing a baby-pink Puma dress and lots of gold rings, came up to us outside the birds of prey area and asked me what tan brand I had used on the girls and how many coats, as she 'loved its glow'.

The day was fairly uneventful although, during the drive through, a monkey pulled a windscreen wiper from a car in front then attacked another monkey with it quite violently.

Charles was really disappointed that he wasn't allowed to feed the rhinos but cheered up when Henry bought him an ant farm kit from the gift shop. All in all, a good day.

Sunday 14th June

Fiona is home, having decided Malia didn't rock after all. After two nights on the town, she booked an early flight back home. She's having a day to 'recover' then is going to Devon with her nan. Priceless.

Evening

Had an unexpected guest earlier this evening. The gate chimed just as I was about to get into the shower after cleaning out the chicken coop. When I pressed the intercom, I was met with an unfamiliar older lady dressed rather like the Queen when she's at her Balmoral country retreat.

'Do you have any eggs?!' asked a well-to-do, older voice into the intercom.

'Urm, yes we do,' I answered, a bit confused.

'Good, good. Let me in then. I need three for a cake I am making for the WI,' came the no-nonsense reply. I was a bit taken aback but buzzed the lady in. A few minutes later, the woman appeared at the top of the drive, on foot and pushing an old bike with a basket on the front.

'Dotty, nice to meet you!' she exclaimed as she lent her bike against the stable wall and shook my hand. I offered her a coffee, which seems to be expected here in the country, and she happily accepted.

I soon came to learn that Dotty is a very well-known and respected local figure. Born and raised in the village, she knew all about the history of Puddle-Duck Farm and told me some wonderful stories of when she used to play here as a young girl over 50 years ago with her friend whose parents owned the property at the time.

'You see that opening in the trees over there?' asked Dotty, gesturing to a large space in the hedgerows. 'That used to be an old potting shed many moons ago. My friend and I used to spend our days there, drawing fairies and wildlife. This is a very special place indeed.'

'It certainly is. The potting shed sounds like something my little people would love. Shame it's not here anymore,' I told her.

'You could always get another. Young children love dens; my great-grandchildren are forever building forts and such like.'

Dotty left shortly after with a dozen eggs in her basket, promising to come and visit again soon and bring us some old photos of the farmhouse. Her recollections of the potting shed got me thinking and I now have a new project. I'm going to put a vintage summer-house in the space where the old potting shed used to be and maybe my daughters will be lucky enough to spot some fairies to draw like Dotty did as a young girl.

Friday 20th June

Evening

I found an old vintage summer-house on e-Bay and, with Henry's help, have spent the last few days bringing it back to life. It's an octagonal, wooden structure with a lovely raised roof and Georgian doors and windows. First we sanded and painted the exterior with Farrow & Ball Cooking Apple Green then painted the doors and the interior wooden walls and floor a Farrow's cream. I've ordered a desk and some animal and fairy prints for the wall and a small sofa and some chunky-knit blankets for when the cooler weather comes. I've also got some twinkly fairy lights for both inside and out. I think it will be a lovely peaceful place for the girls to read and do their homework and, as it looks out onto the meadow and pond, Charles will be able to sit in it and watch the wildlife that he's becoming more obsessed with as each day passes. I think I'll also use it as an office a few afternoons a week when the weather allows so I can admire the garden and have some peace. You don't get much of that at our house; laughter and chaos aplenty but not much peace!

Monday 23rd June

5 p.m.

Just served the girls their supper of slow-baked jacket potatoes with tuna and melted cheese in their summer-house which is now called The Fairy Hut. The hut has been a huge hit with the girls and given them a base out of the living rooms and their bedrooms which always triggers a 'that's my stuff, don't touch it' row.

Charles isn't as keen on the new addition to the garden, saying he prefers to be outside watching the animals. He said, 'I can get a better view of wildlife if I sit out in the mud.'

Edward said the hut is too girly and prefers sitting in the oak tree by the stables. I drew the line at climbing up the tree to hand him his jacket potato as he requested this evening though because I'm not a fan of heights.

Friday 27th June

11 p.m.

PTA members' summer supper at the local pub. All six members including me came plus Robert, the head teacher. The Fox is a real old-fashioned country pub with old Guinness pictures and brass shire-horse badges hung on the wall in between the black wood beams. It's a really quirky building with lots of 'mind your head' signs to warn you of the low ceiling heights and dogs sleeping by their owners' feet while they eat a bar meal in the restaurant.

The bar staff had made a large table for us by pushing several smaller wooden tables together. Amanda, Clair and Quinn, who had arrived before me, had already cracked open a bottle of wine by the time I had sat down and had a look at the menu.

'What are you going to have, Alice?' asked Quinn, picking up his menu.

'I'm not sure yet. I still feel a bit off-colour so I fancy some comfort food,' I replied, still studying the main courses.

'You should try the sausages and mash, Alice. I love the onion gravy here,' said Amanda, joining in the conversation.

'Oh, thanks, babes! What are you ordering, Rob, hun?' Quinn asked Robert as he returned to the table from the bar carrying a pint of bitter for himself and handed what looked to be a large gin and tonic to Quinn.

'I had a lovely bit of steak last time so will be having a sirloin. Would you like a drink, Alice?' Robert asked, spotting me now sitting at the table. I thanked him but said I'd already got myself a sparkling water as I came in.

The waitress came over holding a notepad and pen and took our orders. Everyone decided to try the night's special which happened to be the local organic sausages with cheese and chive mash that Amanda had recommended a few moments before with the exception of Robert who stuck with the sirloin steak. Quinn called the waitress back as he decided to cancel his sausage special order and join Robert and have a steak and chips. He then called the poor waitress back again and asked, 'Can you add a cheeky basket of onion rings to my order as well, hun? Thanks, babes.'

I was still not feeling too great and so left most of my meal but it didn't go to waste as, after eating his own 16-ounce steak, chips and 'cheeky onion rings', Quinn lent over to my plate and declared, 'Waste not want not,' and began spooning dollops of mash and chunks of sausage into his mouth in between gulps of his G&T.

'Right! Who's coming into town?' asked a flushed-faced Clair. Everyone else was all for it. I wanted an early night so offered to drop them all off in town to save them a huge taxi fare before heading home.

'Cheers, babes. Yes, that's brill if you can drop us in town. I won't be staying out for long mind. Someone needs to promise me you won't let me get too pissed. I'm like Cinderella and must home before midnight!' Quinn said, grinning.

Amanda drained her wine glass and then turned to Quinn, took his hand and said, 'I will look after you, Quinn. You're safe with me!'

It always makes me laugh how people who usually cannot abide each other become so friendly after a few drinks. The world would be a much friendlier place if everyone was always half cut on house red.

An hour and a half later, I'd dropped my brilliant if slightly strange mix of new friends off in our closest town and then had taken a slow drive home, still laughing to myself as I thought back to hearing Robert shout, 'COME ON, SQUAD! WHO WANTS SOME TEQUILA?' as he led the way to Shotz, a heaving bar on the market square.

On the drive home, I thought back to this time last year and how I didn't know this great group of people and had never set eyes on Puddle-Duck Farm or my Daisy, Nancy, William and the other new members of my family.

I smiled to myself thinking about tomorrow. Our life was about to change again. As I kicked off my shoes and walked into the kitchen, I was met by a smiling Henry who I'd called on my way home on my hands-free. He had managed to get the children all asleep while I was out then had run me a warm bath and put my fluffy dressing down on the heated towel rail, waiting for me to snuggle into when I got out. Men like him are hard to come by.

Saturday 28th June

11 a.m.

By the sounds of it, Amanda didn't do a very good job of looking after Quinn last night.

'Hello, did you have a good night?' I asked as I answered my mobile after seeing Quinn's name pop up on the screen.

'Well, yes and no. It didn't end that well. The last thing I remember was downing Apple Sourz and dancing to Beyoncé with Rob until I was woken up by the manager of Londis!'

'The manager of Londis? Who is the manager of Londis? And why were they waking you up?' I asked, confused.

Henry also stopped reading his paper and listened in with interest.

'I didn't catch her name but she woke me up because I was leaning against the shutter and she needed to raise it to open the shop!' Quinn replied.

'What?' I laughed.

'Yeah, I know. Not my best moment, hun. Like I say, one minute I was having a ball dancing to "Single Ladies" with Apple Sourz dribbling down my chin, the next I was being poked with a shopping basket at six in the morning outside Londis. I woke up with a right start, still holding a half-eaten kebab and an unopened can of dandelion and burdock!'

Henry erupted into laughter, shaking his head before going back to his paper.

'You must have been in a right mess. What did Richard say?' I asked through tears of laughter.

'I know, babes, I was in a bad way. I must have been because I can't stand dandelion and burdock! Richard has been brilliant. He's gone out to get me some Lucozade and a packet of Haribo to aid my recovery,' he said, joining in with my laughter before adding, 'I blame Amanda. She was supposed to be keeping me in line, although I won't hold it against her. From what Clair texted this morning, she was in a pretty bad way herself. Clair said she had to phone her husband, Roger for a lift home after Amanda got so shit faced that she got them kicked out for slurring, "Who wants to feel these?" while flashing her tits at the bouncers. They were going to give them a second chance until Amanda licked one of their faces!'

'Oh my God!' I said, still cracking up.

'You haven't heard the best of it yet! Amanda then declared in the car that she was really, really desperate for the toilet. They couldn't stop as they were on the motorway so Roger emptied out his side-door holder and managed to find a bag for life. Rather than Amanda piss herself, Clair passed her the carrier bag and instructed her to have a wee in it while crouched down on the back seat, which would have been bad enough but Amanda was so far gone, she got confused and thought Clair meant wee on the seat and then sit on the bag after she had finished! Roger is furious by all accounts as he's only had the Volvo since January. He said he partly blames himself though for not paying extra for leather,' said Quinn, who was now howling with laughter.

4 p.m.

Had been looking forward to today for the last few months. All ten of us Babyladys arrived at the appointment just after lunch. We had a short wait in the reception area where Henry and I took it in turns to repeatedly ask the children to 'sit down and stop touching things' then a petite Indian lady with sleek, glossy hair and a big smile came out and called my name.

'Alice Babylady, would you like to come through?' she asked, gesturing to a nearby door.

All of us stood up and scurried into the small, dark room. The children sat on the floor while Henry took a seat on the chair next to the reclined bed. The lady looked at all the children and smiled before saying, 'Take your time to get comfortable and then we can take a look. Who is excited?'

Everyone, including Henry and me, raised a hand. The woman giggled and then took a seat next to the bed where I was now reclining. After a tense few minutes, in which even the children were quiet as mice, staring at the screen, the lady broke the silence.

'Congratulations! Everything looks perfect. Would you like to know what you're having?' she asked, looking at me and then Henry and the children.

We all said, 'Yes!' in union.

She turned to us and said in an upbeat voice, 'It's a little boy!'

The girls all clapped and Edward and Charles, who were hoping for another brother so they will be less outnumbered, happily shouted, 'Yesss!'

The lady laughed and continued, 'And the dates from the last scan are bang on. This little man is due to make an appearance on December the 24th. A Christmas baby! How wonderful! And you're planning a home birth, aren't you? Now that could be interesting!'

We have a very exciting few months ahead, our first full winter at the farm, Sarah's wedding in Scotland, and a Christmas baby!

Contact the Author

Thank you for reading this book and hope you enjoyed it. I would be extremely grateful if you could leave a review on Amazon, even just one word would be brilliant (hopefully a positive word!).

To be among the first to hear of the publication of my sequels please join my mailing list now via my website (no details needed other than your email address).

I'd love to hear from you and am happy to answer questions you may have. Please get in touch with me by:

Email: hellothebabylady@yahoo.com
Instagram: www.instagram.com/The_baby_lady_
Blog: www.thebabylady.co

I look forward to hearing from you.

Alice Babylady

The Baby Lady Loves

Below are a selection of brands and small shops I genuinely love and believe in.

Fearne and Rosie

Reduced sugar jams and no added sugar sauces made on a family farm in the heart of the Yorkshire Dales. My little people love making homemade pizzas with their Tomato Ketchup, and you cannot beat Fearne and Rosie's Strawberry Jam with juicy bits on toasted fresh bread for breakfast. Rachel, the founder, promises no junk in any of her products. This is a business where the term 'made with love' really applies.

https://fearneandrosie.co.uk

Instagram: @fearne_and_rosie

My Hummy UK

Beautifully crafted teddy bears that aid sleep for babies and children using the wonders of white noise. I was very lucky to be gifted two of these special bears from their range (Fleur and

Pearl) and they work so well. I have even used them to comfort new-born puppies. The bears have a variety of sounds ranging from hair dryer to heart beat, all of which can be controlled from your smart phone where you can set it to sleep sensor or a non-stop mode, as well as many other options. These bears have been a game changer for me and I get much more sleep because of them. Thank you to Kirsty at My Hummy for introducing us to them.

https://shop.myhummy.co.uk
Instagram: @myhummyuk

Star and Snuggles

The apron baby bath towel made from bamboo, and star shaped baby travel wraps. I was gifted the apron bath towel and it's a genius design. The wrap is a metre wide and has an apron style neck piece that leaves both your hands (and chin!) free as you lift the child out of the bath. It's very luxurious. The range of star shaped car travel wraps come in winter and summer additions, and have three and five point harness points and sizes from new-born to 18 months.

https://starsandsnuggles.co.uk
Instagram: @star_snuggles

Eco By Naty

Eco by Naty supply biodegradable and environmentally friendly baby, skincare and feminine products. I have used this brand for nappies, wipes, and pull ups for many years after a well-known brand gave one of my children a bad rash from the chemicals in its nappies. Eco by Naty do not use chemicals in their products, are kind to the environment whilst not compromising on performance. Anyone who would like to try any of these products can use code THEBABYLADY15 at checkout on their website to receive a 15% discount.

https://www.naty.com

Instagram: @ecobynaty

Skippy Lou

Pastel and classic designed zippy sleep suits made from 100% organic cotton. These are so practical with the zip up design and they also look beautiful. Skippy Lou kindly sent me some of these, along with some teething rings. All of the products are so well made and come in little canvas bags so make lovely gifts.

https://skippylou.co.uk

Instagram: @skippyloubaby

Piggy Paint UK

We love a little pamper in our house, so my girls had great fun in trying out some nail polish that was gifted to them from Piggy Paint UK. These polishes are great for children as they are water based, non-toxic, and have a hypoallergenic formula so they are safe for everyone. Plus they have no odour. Our favourite colour is Fairy Fabulous. You can see photos of my girls trying out the colours on my Instagram account.

Nipper and Co

Organic herbal infused blends. Marina, the company owner, is a qualified Agronomist, as well as being a mum, and has combined her knowledge with her Croatian roots to create a very special selection of blends, that not only taste delicious, but also have amazing well-being benefits. Marina has focused on providing customised blends for use during pregnancy, nursing, and colic. Within the range there are also carefully constructed blends focused on relaxation and sleep. I love all the blends but the Wake Me Up Brew is my favourite, as the energy boosters help me beat the afternoon slump I feel some (every!) day.

Harry and Rose

I love this multi-award winning luxury skin care range for babies and children, and they are my favourite bath time products for my little people, alongside Eco by Naty. Harry and Rose are a UK based company that uses natural and organic ingredients like sweet almond, aloe vera, cotton seed, chamomile, and coconut, and so they are gentle on delicate skin and they smell good enough to eat (you can't actually eat them so please don't try!). I was initially gifted a gift box called the baby bonding gift set from the company (thank you guys!) and I now buy the whole range every month. The body lotion is my favourite and I use it twice a day on myself, as I love the smell and texture. It's so comforting.

https://harryandrose.com

Instagram: @harryandrose

Ruby and Len

Amanda is one of my Instagram friends and is a very talented designer and creator of vintage home-made accessories. She recently sent Etta and Agatha some bespoke eye masks in a sheep design. There are some lovely designs over on her etsy page for children and adults, including the sheep design my girls have. All the items are hand made with such care. They are very special and make wonderful gifts. Thank you Amanda for the gifts, the girls use them every night and they're still going strong!

https://www.etsy.com/uk/shop/rubyandlen

Instagram: @rubyandlen

My Little Owl

Leonie makes bespoke bibs and teething bunnies in so many different designs; from ponies to dinosaurs, Christmas to Halloween. There are endless choices and they are all hand made in the UK. My favourites are the autumn vintage fox duo, which was gifted to us, and we love them. Leonie has hundreds of designs available. She is a lovely approachable lady and so also welcomes bespoke orders if you have a particular fabric or size in mind.

https://mylittleowl.co.uk

Instagram: @my_little_owl_bibs

Knit By Lesley

If you are looking for bespoke luxury knitwear have a peep at Lesley's Instagram page. Lesley designs and makes beautiful items for babies, children, and adults using Merino, Silk, and Cashmere Yarns. I have ordered some winter cardigans for my little people, and I also have my eye on the baby bonnets and new-born shawls on the page - just for future reference! Shipping is worldwide. You can contact Lesley directly via Instagram, she's so lovely and will be happy to help with any custom order requests.

Instagram: @knitbylesley

Doodle Pop – Bespoke Artwork

Doodle Pop came about when Louise was pregnant with her third baby, Gabriel. She designed a large birth announcement doodle which she planned to lay him on and share his arrival to the world.

At the time, Louise had also designed an initial doodle for her daughter, Poppy, and so many of her followers on Instagram encouraged her to set up an Etsy Shop and take commissions. So she did and since then she has had the pleasure and honour to draw hundreds of personalised doodles for all different occasions.

In December 2017, Gabriel was tragically born sleeping; Louise used her art work almost as a therapy in the months which followed, as well as working on different projects to fundraise for charities which support families who sadly never get to take their babies home.

Each doodle Louise creates is unique and designed to be a special gift for someone. Some of the pieces Louise has had the honour to create have been to remember babies, celebrate the birth of a little one, wedding, birthday, christening, anniversary gifts-each one full of doodles especially for the person it is designed for. They are a wonderful keepsake and way to celebrate or remember a special occasion. Louise has also helped me in initially contacting Tommys The Baby Charity to set up donations from The Baby Lady Diaries series, and also in reading the early version of this book, so thank you Louise for all your support. x

Instagram: @louiseslittlecorner @_doodle_pop_

Etsy   Shop: https://www.etsy.com/uk/market/doodle_pop_store

Acknowledgements

I will try and keep this short but I will probably fail. Firstly thank you to my Babylady family and friends (even you Beryl!) as without you there wouldn't be a book. My husband deserves a medal as well as a big thank you for putting up with me for the last six months so thank you darling I love you. My twelve little people thank you for not giving a single shit if I wrote this book or not, but allowing me to share our lives - I love you all. Jacky Donovan and Victoria Twead thank you for all the kindness and support during the early stages of this book. My A team - Kate, Vikki, and Jaime, my brilliant and clever friends - your help, laughter and advice has been invaluable, a huge thank you to each of you. And finally, my Instagram chat group girlies - we are all so different but I am glad to know you all.

About the Author

Alice is now a full time writer and lives in a shabby but completely magical farmhouse nestled deep in the English countryside with her husband and their twelve children under thirteen along with an ever growing menagerie of animals.

Printed in Great Britain
by Amazon